GRACI LOWE

Tomorrow A Mystery

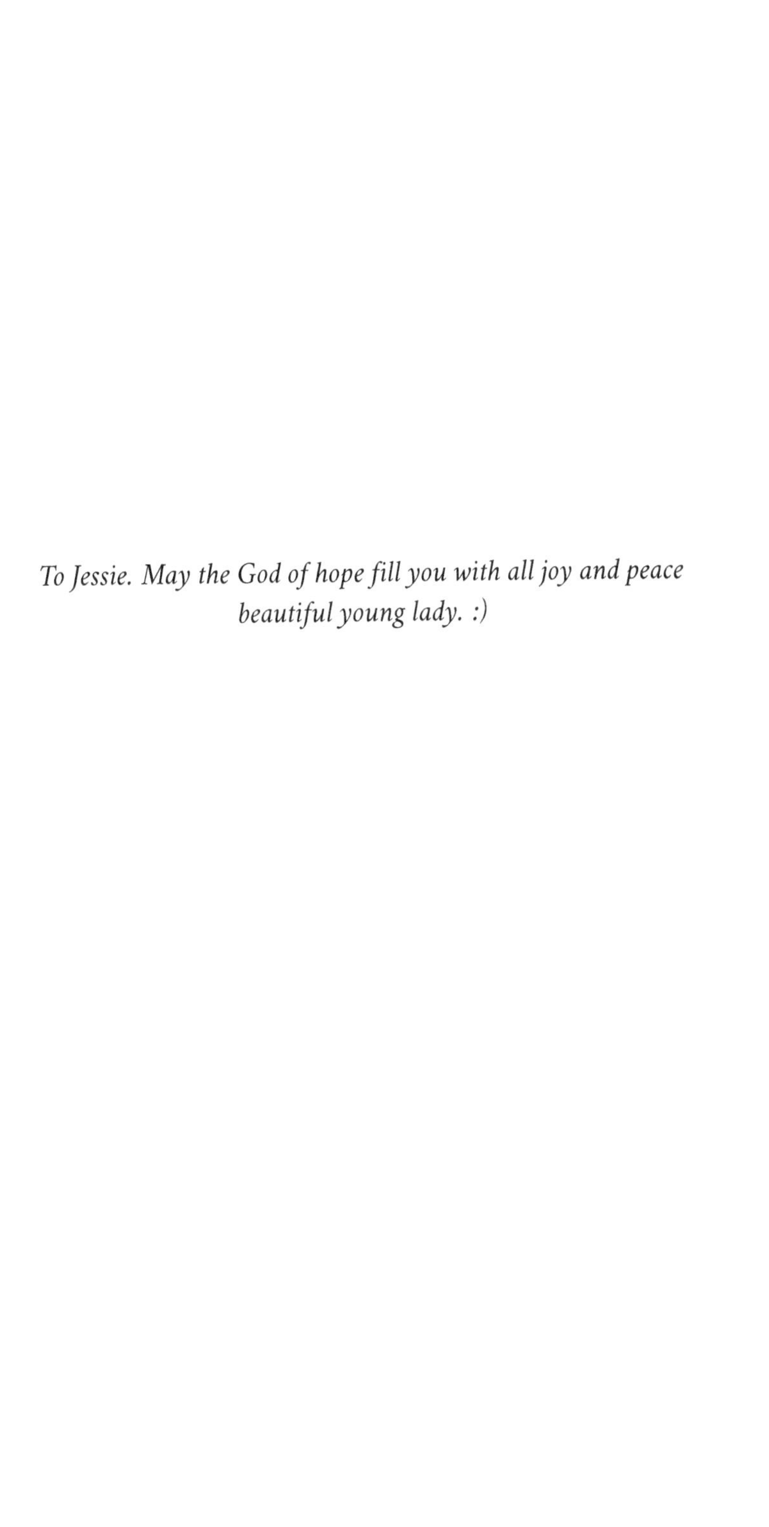

To Jessie. May the God of hope fill you with all joy and peace beautiful young lady. :)

Contents

Note to Reader

Dear Reader,

If you read my previous book, *Yesterday is History*, or if you read the "note to reader" on the first page, got bored, threw the book under your bed, never to be found again, then you would know that I wrote about dreams. Dreams that make you want to do something great. Dreams that make you raise the stakes just a little higher for yourself so that you can do the fantastic things you're capable of. Well in this little reader's note, I'm going to talk about reality. Now you're thinking "Oh great. The reality that awful stuff like murder, abuse, unbearable debt, racism, and countless other things are in the world. That the world is scary and is 'dark and getting darker.'" And you're saying it in your deepest, most Darth Vader like voice, or…at least…I am. Well, no. I hate that this is what people see as the picture of "reality". It's as if you avoid the word during family reunions, along with politics, sports opinions, etc. so that you can continue to have a pleasant time. Well actually, in "reality" all that stuff isn't "reality" at all. Now, hang with me. Yes, these horribly hard things happen, but they are not the "realities of life". Boy, do I hate that phrase. Does it show? We Christians refer to these things as "worldly". All of that is "this too shall pass" material. Believe me, I'm not trying to make it sound less terrible or scarring. I'm trying to make it sound temporary and forgivable. Now, how much hope would it give you to know that in the back of your mind, some powerful being, who loves you more than life itself, is going to one day erase everything bad? Reader, all those horrible things that people are warning us about (debt, abuse, racism, etc.) are so important. They help us know that the world needs our dreams. That the people around us need someone in their life with childlike faith and a soul abounding in hope. Now, let's figure out what reality is. Paul, from the Bible, says that even when this world passes away, faith, hope, and love will remain. The greatest of these being love. Now, how much more real can you get? I want the realities of my life to be so real that they'll last forever. Are you willing to accept a challenge? Make a list of realities that will help you, not chase your dreams, but catch them. Or, maybe go even further by adding to Paul's list. Faith, hope, love, and… .stories?

I hope you enjoy your book Reader.

Aim high!

~Graci

One

Summer Turned to Fall

Trevor woke up. He spent a few moments in the incredible fogginess between sleep and awake, dreading the moment when he remembered what day it was. Sooner than he wished, he remembered. He had to leave in a matter of minutes. He groaned as he pulled the covers off of him. Summer was over. Junior year of college started the very next day. He had spent the majority of his summer break at his grandparents' house. Katherine and Ron Sanders, also known as Grandma and Grandpa, had been the parents that Trevor never really had.

Sure, he wasn't an orphan but he had never felt the nurturing from his parents that every other child seemed to have. His parents divorced shortly after he was born. He was raised by his father most of the time. His dad had never taken him fishing, never thrown a ball with him, never told him that he loved him. Frankly, Trevor wasn't quite sure if he did. The separation he felt from his dad influenced the person he was as a child and teenager. But, he had changed and he had no intention of remembering who he was before that change. Unfortunately for him, they were times his father constantly wanted to bring up.

It seemed like his dad always had a different plan for him. He wanted him to remain the defensive, trust no-one, city kid who he had raised, while Trevor just wanted to have friends. His father was not happy in the least that his son was going to college in a completely different part of the country. Trevor never wanted to hurt anybody's feelings, he simply felt that to be the person that God wanted him to be, he had to take a break from all the anger and resentment he had been receiving from his father his entire life.

His whole life had been so complicated. He always felt so alone. Like he had to fend for himself. Like no-one cared enough to fight for him. Except at Grandma and Grandpa's house.

He walked to the kitchen where his grandmother was making breakfast.

"Last day here," said Katherine, "I thought we would have pancakes."

"Thank you, Grandma," said Trevor as he kissed her on the head.

"Your grandfather should be out in a minute."

"Hon, did we remember to get coffee creamer at the store?" Trevor's grandfather yelled from the bedroom.

"Yes, Ronnie. Come down here and say goodbye to your grandson before you go to work."

"I will," he answered. "Hey, where's that package we were going to give Trevor?"

"Attic hon. In that back corner."

"Oh Grandma, you didn't have to get me anything," Trevor said, wondering what it could be.

"Don't worry, we didn't," his grandmother answered with an almost mischievous gleam in her eye.

"Found it!" Ron yelled from the attic.

Trevor's grandfather walked down the stairs carrying a box with stickers and stamps from all over the world on it. He made his way into the kitchen, holding the box by its sides. He reached it to Trevor without saying a word.

"What is this?" he asked.

"Open it," Katherine said.

He opened it before saying, "It's full of letters."

"I wrote those to different people when I was in the army. Everything from basic training to the day I bowed out is inside this box," Ron said. "I thought they could be useful to you."

"Grandpa, these are your letters. I don't want to take them from you!" Trevor argued.

"Is that a true statement, Trevor Foster?" Ron asked, smiling.

"No sir. I would love to read them-"

"Well then, here you go. Now, I have to go if I don't want to be late for work. Bye Kat," He said when he kissed his wife. "I will see you next time Trevor."

"You too, Grandpa. And, thanks for the letters."

"Anytime."

Ron smiled and left the house. Shortly after, Trevor packed all his things into his car. He was not ready to leave. He hugged his grandmother, got into his car, and drove off. He had to keep reminding himself that he was driving, for his head was so full of thoughts. Thoughts of his friends who he had not seen in months. He thought about school and his girlfriend. How had summer ended so quickly? It was as if he hadn't even seen it go bye. The flowers were no longer there. The trees had gone from green to all the different colors of fall. The world seemed to turn from summer to autumn in a matter of minutes.

After the two hour drive, Trevor pulled into the parking lot of his dorm. His group of friends was standing on the curb waiting for him. Olivia, his girlfriend, Carlos, his best friend, and Abby, his cousin. He got out of the car with a growing smile on his face. Olivia ran and hugged him.

"Trevor! I missed you so much!" she said in his favorite Texas accent.

"I missed you too!" he answered.

"Amigo! It has been so long!" Carlos said as he shook his hand.

"Carlos! It's so good to see you, buddy!" Trevor answered. "How was your family holding up in Cuba?"

"Mi familia es fantástica! And Cuba es as beautiful as ever."

"Glad to hear it," Trevor said. "And how's my favorite cousin?"

"I'm your favorite?" Abigail said, smiling. "Should I take a bow?"

"Just come here!" he said as he reached to hug her.

Trevor had missed his friends so much. Seeing them almost made it worth it to go back to school. Almost.

Trevor sighed. The worst part about autumn: school. Another year of useless school that he didn't care about and wasn't good at. Who cares about stupid math problems that he'll never see again or use those stupid formulas. Trevor was so sick of the whole "back to school" scene.

He brought all of his stuff into his dorm with the help of his friends. He began unpacking a few of his clothes and started finding his school supplies.

After a few hours, he decided to take a walk across campus. He thought about the months ahead. It was rare that Trevor spent this much time within his own thoughts, but this year was going to be different. This year he went from a child to an adult. This year he must decide what he wants to do. He must decide who he wants to be.

Finally, he found it. The little stone bench next to the library where he had sat and thought for the last two years. He sat down and looked out at the beautiful view of the sky against the brick buildings. In a matter of minutes, his cousin walked out of the building holding a few books.

"What are you doing here?" Abby asked.

"I come here probably once a day when school's in session," Trevor said as he fidgeted with his hands.

"Well, it is a very nice bench."

"I thought so. Do you want to sit with me?"

"Sure," Abby sat down and paused before saying, "I can't believe this is my second year of college. Or that you're a junior!"

"Crazy, isn't it."

"Have you decided what you're going to major in yet?"

Trevor rubbed his forehead as he said, "I don't know, Abb. Some people think it's amazing that we have all these options open to us, but I find it overwhelming. I'm not even that good at school."

"Yeah?"

"And I really want to marry Olivia and the most embarrassing part is that I can't until I know I can support her."

"You do? You want to get married?" Abby said with growing excitement.

"Yes! But I can't see a way to do that until I find a steady job and to do that I have to get an education. How do I know that I'm choosing the right major Abby? How do I know that what I'm studying is what I will want to do for the rest of my life."

"Well, I don't think any of us actually know if we're making the right decisions. Just take a leap. If you don't like your chosen study, find a different one. And if you don't like that one, try again. That's what college is Trevor, finding out what you want to do. It's a place to get ideas. Just, don't lose hope. You're an amazing person. You'll figure it out."

"Abby, I can't. It doesn't work that way."

"Don't you have a dream? I know that sounds like a Disney movie, but seriously. You won't get anywhere unless you have somewhere to go. "

"But that's the thing. I don't have a dream. I don't have a clue what I want to do. I don't really know who I am. What if I don't know how to dream?"

"Have you tried hoping?"

"Has anyone ever told you about the real world, Abby? About

how expensive college is? I'm already under a huge weight of debt, changing majors would just add to it."

"Look, you can call me naive and say that my excitement about college is ridiculous, but in my experience, there is nothing naive about having hope. You should try it sometime."

Trevor just looked at his shoes.

"*'Yeah you're right cuz',*" Abby said, trying to imitate Trevor's voice, "Why thank you, Trevor, I appreciate that. *'Oh, that's ok Abby. You're the best cousin ever'.*"

Trevor started to laugh. Something he had needed to do for a while. At that moment, Trevor's phone began vibrating in his pocket. He pulled it out. His dad. Again. He hit decline and shoved the phone right back where he found it.

"Who was that?" Abby asked.

"Oh it-uh-" Trevor hesitated, debating whether or not he should tell the truth, "it was my dad. We're kind of-um-in a fight right now." (Or they'd been in the same fight for the past two years. Unnecessary information, Trevor decided to call it.)

"Oh, well, ok."

There were a few moments of awkward silence before Abby finally said, "Oh, Olivia wanted me to ask you if you were still taking her out tomorrow."

"Yeah. Tell her I'll pick her up for lunch."

"Ok. I love you, Trevor."

"I know you do."

Trevor grabbed her hand as she was walking away, as a way to tell her that he was listening. He didn't know what he would do without Abby. There are some things that you can only talk about to people who know where you've been. Who you were as a child and how much you've changed. He just wished his dad could be more like Abby, maybe see things a little more as she did.

Trevor walked back to his dorm to continue unpacking. He got through a few boxes before seeing the box his grandfather had given him. He took it to his bed and opened it up. The letters were neatly sorted from basic training to his retirement from the army. Trevor decided he'd read the first one. Before hearing his grandfather's story, he never knew how much alike they really were.

Two

Right Choice? Wrong Choice?

8/29/1978

Dear dad,

So, day one of basic training is over. Only fifty-five more to go. Gee, I hope that goes by faster than it sounds it will. I hope you're not still mad at me for giving up that basketball scholarship and not going to college so that I could join the army. I'm beginning to get mad at myself too. Who would sign up for this? My arms are feeling like noodles while my legs are feeling like jello. Passing out has become something that happens hourly and dehydration is a word that's used frequently.

I know when you saw this in the mail, you probably called to mom saying,

"Honey! Ron sent us his first letter from the army! Let's hear how fantastic he's doing!"

And then she probably said something like, "Wait! Don't open it until I get in there! I want to read it too!"

And then you probably opened it with a smile on your face, ecstatic to hear how your little boy is doing. Well, sorry to burst your bubble, dad because it is TERRIBLE here. And when I say TERRIBLE, I mean I should've taken that basketball scholarship when I had the chance. Oh yeah, that's right, I said it. I was wrong and you were right. That's how miserable I am. I'm admitting defeat. I mean, I might as well. I feel like I was run over by a bulldozer at this second.

This is about the worst place on earth that I could ever go and probably ever will go. At least I'm getting paid to sweat my guts out and puke all over the base.

Drill sergeant Samuels is a jerk and calls me a failure at least once every two minutes. The food here looks amazing. Too bad I've lost my appetite and even the smell of food makes me nauseated. I dread tomorrow. And to think that when I signed up I thought it'd be fun. Way to crush my hopes and dreams, drill sergeant Samuels.

I don't know how much longer I'm going to be able to take this. It is so hot in my barracks. I'm sweating through my clothes. I don't know how much we ran today, but let me tell you it felt like four thousand, seven hundred, and thirty-six miles. Oh, it was awful.

Technically I'm not even supposed to be writing this but it's not like Drill sergeant Samuels could yell at me any louder. What? Do you think I'm over exaggerating?

Picture this: I'm running circles on the track, not that hard for me because of basketball, and the entire group of training soldiers is running with me. Drill sergeant Samuels begins to run beside me, as I'm running as fast as I can, and yells,

"WHAT IS THIS, A GIRL SCOUT COOKIE MEETING? WE'RE TRYING TO GET YOU READY FOR COMBAT, YA SISSY! GET THOSE KNEES UP!"

And so I say, "Yes, drill sergeant," through stolen breaths because I feel like a hippopotamus is sitting on my chest.

"LOOK! I'M RUNNING CIRCLES AROUND YOU, SANDERS!" he yells loud enough to make my ears bleed. And yes he was running circles around me. "LOOK, TROOPS! APPARENTLY, SANDERS DOESN'T KNOW HOW TO RUN! HE LOOKS LIKE A CLOWN OUT HERE! RIGHT EVERYBODY?"

And the entire troop says (as they're supposed to), "YES DRILL SERGEANT!"

"YOU DON'T KNOW HOW TO RUN, DO YOU SANDERS?"

"Yes, drill sergeant."

So, in reality, the army hires people to run laps in a state that feels like a desert so that your drill sergeant can call you names and say awful things about you. AND I HAVE TO AGREE WITH HIM! The only thing I've been allowed to say for the past twenty-four hours is "Yes drill sergeant". If I disagree when the drill sergeant calls me a girl scout, I'm going to have to stay at week one of basic for the rest of my life.

Oh, joy. Apparently, drill sergeant Samuels is getting a megaphone tomorrow so that we "girl scouts" can hear him better. So, I think it may have been the biggest mistake in the history of my entire life to even think of joining the army. In conclusion, the army stinks and I don't know how it could possibly get worse but, hey, it's the seventies, anything is possible.

Oh, I almost forgot. I know mom will be wondering. No, I have not made any friends yet. I haven't had enough minutes in my day that weren't spent, passing out, puking, trying to get my breath back, or better yet, getting the invisible elephant off of my chest. Maybe this is a sign that I'm not where I'm supposed to be. I mean, you guys know how much of a people person I am! A guy who was doing sit-ups beside me goes,

"Wow, you've got some real stamina when you're doing sit-ups. You practice often?"

And you know what I said? I said, "You're welcome," then I cringed and it went downhill from there.

I started trying to revive myself by saying, "I mean, thank you. I blayed a lot of plastic ball."

Nope. I didn't accidentally spell that wrong. I actually told the guy that I blayed plastic ball. I'm a people person dad! I'm usually so good at this! The army has ruined me. But, I mean, I can't blame the inability to speak English to a person completely on myself. I was out of breath and everyone was slurring their words pretty bad. I'm probably just way overthinking this.

The guy said his name was Fred. He said that he and some

of his buddies were thinking about playing football tomorrow in this grassy area beside the barracks. I haven't decided if I'm going to go or not yet.

I miss Indiana. I miss knowing people and saying hi in the middle of the grocery store. I miss going to church every Sunday and knowing everybody. Wow, this sounds ridiculous.

I guess what I'm trying to say is, it's so hard to make decisions like this. Maybe this was the wrong one for me. What was I thinking? I'm a basketball player! I'm no soldier. I don't have a clue of how they're going to make a soldier out of me. How are we supposed to know if we're making the right choices? How are we supposed to know if what we're doing is going to be what makes us happy? Is there a sign that comes along at some point? Because right now, I'm not seeing it. Maybe one day I'll figure out if this was the right choice.

I have to go. Drill sergeant Samuels said to get in bed. I just can't wait to get up at four in the morning. (That was said sarcastically if you wanted to know.)

Your son,
Ron Sanders

Three

Benny's Waffle House

Trevor laid in bed, staring at the bottom of Carlos' top bunk mattress. He dreaded getting up because getting up meant he had to start the day. Getting up meant he had to start the week, which meant he had to start school. School to Trevor was an alternative way to spell procrastination, failure, stress, and the disappointment of his father.

Carlos threw his head over the side of the bunk to see if Trevor had woken up. "Hola, amigo!"

Trevor looked at Carlos, then back to the mattress above him. "Hey, buddy."

"What are you going to do today?"

"Oh, I thought I'd go to the grocery store, unpack my boxes, take Olivia to Benny's, then start digging a hole to China so I don't have to map out my entire life."

"You are still nervous about sign up week, yes?"

"Oh, you could tell?"

"Well, amigo, you only say you are going to dig a hole to China when you are not wanting to do something. Usually something important," Carlos said as he got off of his bunk.

"I guess I have been using that line for a while."

"Si. Since the eighth grade."

"You're right, pal," Trevor said as he began to get up. "But you used it that one time too!"

"Amigo, if you were in my position, you would understand."

"Carlos, you put me in that position when you said I should 'voy a por ello' and ask Olivia out!"

"Si," Carlos answered, "Pero, your cousin is gorgeous! You know that I become nervioso when I try to talk to her."

"And Olivia isn't gorgeous?"

"Oh no, Amigo! What I meant was…I was going to say…Ah, ayúdame, Jesús."

"I'm just saying, you've liked Abby as long as I've liked Olivia. Olivia and I are going on a year and Abby doesn't even know you're interested. I say you're chicken."

"Maybe I am," Carlos shugged. "Or maybe I'm waiting for the right momento to woo her with my charm and manliness."

"Whatever you say, man," said Trevor laughing. "I've got to get ready to pick Olivia up. I'll see you in a little while, Carlos."

"Si, señor. See you later."

Trever got into his little silver car, drove halfway across campus, pulled into the parking lot of the girls' dorm, and honked his horn. He waited in his car for his girl to come out. That's when he received a call from his father. He hit decline-for the third time today.

A few minutes later, Olivia came out in her signature jeans and cowgirl hat, with her brown hair in those beautiful fat curls.

"And how might you be doin' this fine evenin', my lady?" said Trevor in his best country accent.

"Oh now don't make fun of my Texas roots. I feel no shame, sir."

"Right, sorry," Trevor said as he kissed her. "You ready?"

"I'm ready."

About five minutes later, Trevor and Olivia arrived at Benny's waffle house. A place to which they had been on many occasions. It was dirty and disorganized but it had a sort of charm about it that no other place had. Nobody came for the food, it wasn't that good. Everyone came more for the weird ambiance. There were several of those weird, one of a kind objects hanging on the walls, and Trevor and Olivia had no idea what any of them were.

He was quiet and toyed with the food sitting on the plate in front of him. Olivia tried to keep the conversation alive but was failing in her efforts. Finally, she said,

"Trevor, are you doin' alright?"

"Yeah, just thinking about this week. I'm sure I sound pathetic and like I haven't thought about this at all, but I have! This is a pretty important decision in my life. I just don't know what to major in."

"Yeah, I understand."

"I have to think about who I'm going to be and what I want to do. I have to think about getting a job so that I can provide for myself."

"Yeah."

"And then I have to think about you and the kids." Pause. Oops. Trevor cringed.

Olivia blinked a few times before she said, "You have to think about who?"

"Not that we have to have kids!" Trevor shifted in his seat. "I just think if we *were* to get married, and if we *were* to have kids, I would need a profession to support the hypothetical kids that we might not have…in the future."

Olivia smiled. "Yeah?"

"I just think, life is full of decisions. Good ones, bad ones, ones that need a lot of thought. How can I explain this?" Trevor paused for thought, "It's like that game with the block tower! You know, the one where you pull the blocks out one at a time."

Olivia was utterly confused. "Jenga?"

"Yeah!"

"Mhmm…" Olivia said with her eyebrow raised.

"And you're just going along and every decision is one of those blocks you have to pull out, with your life being the tower. And you're just pulling out block after block after block. Olivia, if I pull out the wrong block, the whole tower will come crashing down! If I make the wrong decision, my life will come crashing down!"

Olivia put her hand on his, smiling and laughing occasionally as she did. "Trevor! Listen to yourself, baby! Your life is not a game of Jenga. Your life is amazin' because of who you are! You have Carlos and Abby and me." Trevor looked down at his food. Olivia grasped his hand a little tighter. "Look at me, baby! You don't have to worry about supportin' me or the hypothetical children. All you have to worry about is what classes you want to take for the next little bit. You are not amazin' because you find a good job or because you get good grades. You're amazin' because of who you are. Trevor Foster. You're Abby's favorite cousin. You're the reason she came to this college. You're Carlos' best friend. You're the reason HE came to this college. You're my boyfriend, the man I want to spend the rest of my life with. Don't you see? You're an inspiration just because you're you."

"Wow. Your boyfriend sounds like a swell guy," Trevor said, slightly shocked.

"And that's without a major," Olivia said smiling.

Trevor went through the rest of his day with a new thought process. Maybe he could relax a little bit more. Maybe he'd just go home and look over all the classes with a new point of view. He still had six more days. He'd figure it out. He was determined.

Trevor decided he would turn to a man who was going through something very similar. Or, at least, he was, in 1978.

Four

Black-Eyed Football

9/1/1978

Dear mom,

So, I decided to play in that football game with Fred and all his friends that I wrote to dad about last time. I had a lot of fun. It actually made me think a little differently about this whole Army thing. I mean, I'm not about to go telling my future children that they should do it, but it's not a complete and total disaster.

Anyway, I decided I would play football with Fred and his buddies. We were throwing, tackling, yelling, and having such a blast. We weren't even keeping score. About twenty minutes into the game, drill sergeant Samuels came to us. We all got off the grass and stood in a line, saluting in front of him. He gestured his hands in such a way that we knew he meant 'at ease'. He stood in front of us and said,

"I'd like to play with you boys if that's ok."

We all looked at each other thinking the exact same thing. 'Drill sergeant Samuels actually wants to have fun? Does he even know what that means?'

Finally, Fred said, "Yes, drill sergeant. My team needs a quarterback. Anderson keeps fumbling."

"No, I-" Anderson started arguing, before realizing he was in the presence of a drill sergeant, and shutting up.

"Anderson, full back! Drill sergeant Samuels, quarterback! Everybody else, same positions!" Fred yelled, getting into his position. "AND HIKE!"

We practiced several different plays and had a lot of fun. I got the not very coveted job of trying to get to drill sergeant Samuels before he got to throw the ball to one of his teammates. I got voted in because nobody else wanted the job of tackling the sergeant. Hey, somebody's got to be the man, right?

We had been playing for a while, and just like every other time, the ball went to drill sergeant Samuels, and he started looking for someone to throw it to. I ran past the opposing team's players, dodging as I went. I finally got to the drill sergeant, still looking for someone to receive the ball. I lunged and tackled him. What I didn't realize was that during all the commotion, my shoulder had slammed right onto my drill sergeant's eye when I tackled him.

I got up and looked down at him. He was blinking and shaking his head from side to side, probably trying to put his eye back into its socket. I reached out my hand to help him up as the rest of the soldiers began coming around to see what happened.

"I'm very sorry, sir," I said, hoping I wasn't going to be deported or something.

"That's alright, soldier," he said, touching the skin around his eye, which was quickly turning from red to orange. "Put some strength like that into your physical training, and you'll get through in no time."

I laughed a little and pulled him up. "Does it hurt much?" I asked, still being careful about what I said.

"If nothing else, it'll make me look more threatening to the troops," he answered as he slammed his hand onto my back.

I was pushed forward a little bit by the amount of force drill sergeant Samuels put behind that "pat" on the back. He walked off to try and find some ice. When he was out of sight, Fred and the rest of the guys crowded around me.

"That was awesome!" a guy named Brewster said.

"You think it'll turn black?" another added.

"Oh, there's no doubt."

"That had to hurt! Sanders is a strong dude! And running full speed? Ouch!"

"I've always wanted to cause drill sergeant Samuels pain!" Anderson said slamming his fist into the palm of his hand.

"Anderson! Dude, that's a little dark," Brewster said.

"How good did it feel to give drill sergeant Samuels a black eye?" Fred asked, laughing as he put his hand on my shoulder.

"Well, you know, when somebody is continuously making me mad, he's bound to have it coming to him," I said, shrugging as if the black eye was completely intentional.

"Yeah, he does!" Fred said loud and excitedly.

I intentionally left out the fact that for about a minute, I had been wondering if I was going to be an American citizen for much longer.

We walked back into the barracks and got some water. After that, Fred and I became friends. We're probably going to get hot dogs this evening in our uniforms and see how many girls we can get to say 'thank you for your service' to us.

The blackeyed football game was a couple of days ago, and Fred and the guys are still talking about it. Drill sergeant Samuels' eye is still kind of purple. I honestly thought I was going to be kicked out of the army for injuring a sergeant. My drill sergeant no less.

Anyway, in my last letter, I wasn't sure if being in the army was the right decision for me. Honestly mom, I still don't know. What I do know is that I have been having so much fun in the last couple of days. I mean basic training is still a nightmare and I've passed out about ten more times since the last letter, but I have made some friends and I have been having a lot of fun. Even if this isn't the right decision for me, I am having a really great time.

Sometimes, I think you just have to take a leap of faith. I mean, when God was mapping out the plan he had for my life, He factored in all the wrong turns I was going to take and all the nonsense I was going to get into. Even if this isn't the right decision for me, I'm not saying that it is, but even if it isn't, God will use me wherever I land. My job is to jump.

Wow, this being an adult stuff is complicated! Who knew?

I'm missing you and dad and everyone back in Indiana. Hopefully, seven and a half more weeks will go by quicker than we think. Or quicker than it sounds at least. I can't wait to see you when I graduate. I hope you are doing well.

Your son,
Ron Sanders

Five

Cuban Mechanics

Trevor laughed as he folded the discolored letter and put it back into the box. Maybe his grandfather had a point. If an opportunity arose that Trevor thought interesting, he would take a leap. God will use him wherever he ends up. That's when Carlos' phone rang.

"Ah hola, Fernando…Sí me voy en unos minutos…No, no lo sabía…Sí, hay que hacerlo…Ok. Adiós."

Carlos got off of the phone.

"Amigo, I must go to mi mecanico shop today. I have some things to take care of. Would you like to come?"

Trevor thought about it for a moment. "Um, sure Carlos. I need to get away from college for a little bit anyhow."

The two men got into Carlos' four-door, green pick up truck. They talked while Carlos drove the twenty miles.

They talked about the summer break and what interesting things they were going to do within the year. They talked about new things they were watching on tv. Finally, Carlos asked about Trevor's girl, knowing all the while where the conversation would lead.

"So how was your lunch with Olivia my friend?"

"It was nice. Really nice. I don't know what I'd do without her," Trevor said smiling.

"Muy bien mi amigo," Carlos answered with a bit of sadness in his voice.

"Cough cough, you could have the same with Abby, cough cough," Trevor said with his fist in front of his mouth.

"Amigo, it defeats the purpose of the fake coughing if you say 'cough' instead of making it sound like a cough."

"Hey, I'm just sayin'" Trevor added with his hands in a 'don't shoot' position.

"And besides, cuando el tiempo is right, I will take her some-where."

"Oh sure, sure."

"Oh look, we have arrived," Carlos said in a way that made his friend feel as though he was through with the conversation.

Trevor smiled, laughed, and got out of the car. He looked at the little brick building, painted white, with two garage doors, and the sign above his head with the words 'Cuban Mechanics' written in bold blue letters. Carlos took a breath, straightened his shirt, and went in. This was the hardest thing he had to do as a CEO.

When the door opened, the five 'Cuban mechanics' stopped their work and went to greet their boss. There were four men and one woman, all of which spoke Spanish fluently. Carlos had told Trevor once that he wanted all who worked there to speak Spanish for a reason. When he first immigrated and didn't know English, he felt so alone. He said he wanted his shop to be a place where you could come whether you spoke Spanish or English. He was a big fan of inclusion.

"¡Carlos! Te hemos echado de menos. Ha pasado tanto tiempo," one man said. Trevor recognized him.

"Fernando, isn't it?" Trevor asked, reaching out his hand.

"Si, señor. And you are Trevor, yes?"

He nodded. Carlos moved to the front of the room, cleared his throat, and began talking to his co-workers. Fernando translated for Trevor.

"Hello everyone! I have missed working with all of you. I only have a few months until the autumn semester is over, and then I will be all yours! I cannot wait to get back into my mechanics suit once again. As incredible as it is for me to see all of you, I'm afraid there is something that I need to do. Mr. Hernández, would you step into my office for a moment?"

Although Carlos tried not to make a big deal out of the situation, everyone knew that Hulio Hernández was, unfortunately, getting fired. Trevor felt bad for him but worse for Carlos. 'It must be so awful to have to do that for his job' Trevor thought. While Carlos was in his office, Trevor began talking to Fernando.

"It will be very hard without Hulio here."

"Yeah?" Trevor asked.

"Si. It was hard enough when he was here, but I cannot imagine doing it with one less set of hands."

"Yeah."

"We had to begin putting cars outside for we had no more room."

"Well, that's one of those things that are good and bad at the same time I guess," Trevor answered.

"Si," Fernando said, pausing as though he was considering saying something. Finally, he gave in. "Are you a mechanic, señor?"

"Me?" Trevor asked. "Oh no, no I'm just…I'm," he thought about it for a moment. "Actually, I don't know what I am."

"Let me ask another question," Fernando said. "Would you like to become a mechanic, señor?"

"You know what, Fernando, let me get back to you on that," Trevor said with new thoughts racing in his head. That's when his phone rang. Dad. Again.

Trevor hung up the phone and returned it to his back pocket. At that moment, Carlos came out of his office behind a sad-looking Hulio. Once again, Trevor pitied Carlos. He would hate to be in that man's shoes. Carlos said goodbye to all of his mechanic friends and reminded them once again that he would be back on the job as soon as his semester was over. Carlos and Trevor got back in the truck.

"Carlos?" Trevor asked.

"Yes, amigo?"

"What if I worked there?"

"Worked where? Cuban Mechanics?"

"Yeah. I could major in maintenance and repair. I would take Spanish so that I could talk to everyone. Fernando is stressed out now that Hulio's gone. You guys need an extra set of hands. Carlos! I could work with you! What if I worked there?"

"Well, amigo, I am sure you would do well. It does not pay very much."

"That's ok, buddy!"

"If that is what you want to do amigo, it is ok with me."

"Seriously?"

"Si! It would be fun to work with my best friend outside of the classroom."

"Yeah!"

Maybe Trevor's life wasn't a game of Jenga. Maybe this could work. Maybe he could become a mechanic. He'd sign up tomorrow. This would be great.

Six

The Best Friend

10/26/1978

Dear dad,

I wanted to thank you again for coming to my basic training graduation ceremony. I regret to tell you that that was my favorite day in the entire eight weeks. Though basic was terrible, I am relieved to tell you that I have begun studying communications. I do not communicate with Americans as much as I intercept messages from threats or anybody else using morse code or just regular words. I am in this huge building with a gigantic satellite on top that looks like it dressed up like a golf ball for Halloween. I am very interested in what I've been studying. Fred and Anderson got moved to communications with me so that will be interesting.

What I really wanted to talk to you about though is this girl. I'm not sure if she even knows I'm alive yet. She's got black hair and dark eyes. I told Fred that I liked her and he responded with something that is still making me nervous.

"Ok, you like the black-haired one?"

"Yeah."

"Alright, look at the woman right beside her. Johnson, I think is her name."

"Ok."

"See how they're laughing and talking amongst themselves?"

"Yeah."

"Now that is a best friend," Fred crossed his arms, grinned, and leaned back slightly as if I already knew what he was trying to say.

I paused for a while before I said, "So….?"

"Dude, everybody knows! Best friend is code for you don't stand a chance."

"What?" I said, not understanding in the least little bit.

"Look, as of right now, that girl doesn't need you because her best friend is with her. When she's got her best friend, she has more fun than she does with anybody else. If you want to get to the girl, you have to go through her best friend. Girls…girls are complicated creatures, but once you know how they work," Fred winked, "you might actually stand a chance."

I nodded with the ever-present confused look on my face. Now I was nervous. I had to talk to Johnson and try and ask her if I stood a chance at getting with Brown. I walked over to her.

"Um, excuse me, miss Johnson, could I see you for a moment?" I said as I casually walked away from her friend, avoiding eye contact.

"Yes?" she said, with a tone that was not helping my nervousness. I brought her to the other side of the room.

"Ok, here's the deal," I answered, "I-uh-I really like your best friend and I would really like to take her to a movie but see, there's-uh-there's this thing that my friend told me about. You're her best friend and if you don't like me, she'll hate me, so I really need you to like me."

"What? I don't even know you!"

"Well, that's fair," I said taking a deep breath, preparing to talk as fast as I ever had. Partly because I was nervous and partly because I was desperate. "My name is Ron Lee Sanders. I'm a basketball player from Indiana. I enjoy the company of dogs and I really like to watch sports. I despise school. I was really REALLY glad when I finished basic training. I've been a Christian since I was little. I absolutely hate Mexican food. The salsa makes me want to gag. I'm a football fan, but I was never very good at it. I broke my nose several times in high school and that's why it's got this bump on it. I am an average everyday army man who would really like to take your best friend to a movie. Now you know me. Please, please, Ms. Johnson. I'm begging here."

Johnson crossed her arms and looked at me for a moment. "Won't work," she finally said.

"WHAT? WHY?" I was beyond confused, "Look, Ms. Johnson, if you just say you like me it'll make it so much easier on both of us. Say you like me and I'll go away and have a shot at your friend. Say you like me and you won't have to deal with another one of these terribly awkward interactions. Just say that I can take her out. Please! That's all you have to say and I'll go."

"Katherine loves salsa."

"Katherine? Her name's Katherine?"

"Yup. Katherine Brown and she loves salsa. She eats it right out of the bowl. With a fork. I don't know how she'll feel about dating a salsa hater."

"What?"

"You said in your little speech a second ago that you hated salsa. It won't work."

"Look. If she likes salsa so much…I will eat salsa with her. Now, can I please take Katherine Brown to a movie? Please?" I was on the verge of getting on my knees.

Johnson paused. "Fine. But no more of this 'Ms. Johnson' stuff. I don't like it. I'm Abigail."

"YES!" I said. "Thank you, Abigail. Thank you. I will be paying you back for years!" I began running back to Fred but stopped and said, "Oh! Abigail, put in a good word for me, ok?"

She laughed and said, "Get out of here Sanders!"

I ran to the other side of the room to tell Fred how good I had done.

"I'm going out with Katherine! I'm going out with Katherine!" I said.

"Ron, you haven't asked her yet."

"Yes, I did! I just got finished!" I said.

"No," Fred laughed as he grabbed my shoulders and turned me around so that I saw Katherine. "You haven't asked HER yet."

You know, Fred always seems to have a way of spoiling the moment. All I have to do is ask her. It's fine. It's fine! I can do this. It'll be great. Do you have any advice on this one, dad? I'm really going to need some help. I should go. I have to work in the kitchen today. Yes, dad, I got my first job in the army! I'm washing pots and pans. Somebody has to do it. Anyway, thanks again for coming to my graduation ceremony. And don't forget to give me advice on my situation here.

Your son,

Ron Sanders

Seven

Proposal Perfection

Trevor was so happy. He had stayed up half the night researching which classes he was supposed to take in order to become a mechanic. Carlos secured a position for Trevor for when the semester was over so that he could begin working when he was free. He left his dorm room and ran over to the girls' dorm so that he could tell Abby and Olivia the big news. His mind was racing. Now he had a way to provide for a family. He was officially an adult. He could ask Olivia to marry him!

He finally arrived at the dorm. He knocked on the door as hard as he could and waited for it to be opened. Finally, Abby arrived.

"Oh hey, Trevor!" she said as she gestured for him to come in. "It's been a few days."

"Yeah. Sorry. Well-I-uh-where's Olivia? I need to tell the two of you something."

"Oh, Olivia had a science class. She won't be back for a while."

"Oh, well, I can tell you then. Uh, let's sit…yeah let's sit" He grabbed her hand and brought her to the couch. "Abby, I know what I'm going to do with my life."

"Really? That's great, Trevor! What is it?"

"I'm going to become a licensed mechanic and work at Carlos' shop. It just fell into place! We went down there because Carlos had something to take care of and it turns out they had a job opening! Abby! I can finally ask Olivia to marry me! We can get a house and a dog and a coffee pot and have the whole cliche family life if she wants it."

Abby smiled as big as she ever had. "That's so amazing Trev!"

"And I could be a dad. I'm all grown up now, Abby!"

"I'm so proud of you, Trevor! That's amazing! I've never seen you so happy."

"Well this job means I can finally marry Olivia, and she makes me happy."

"That's so amazing," Abby waited a moment, smiling as she looked down. Then her head shot up and she asked, "Do you have a ring? Can I see it?"

"Ring? What ring? OH SHOOT A RING!" Trevor hopped up and started getting ready to leave.

Abby laughed, "You know what, that doesn't matter. I'm sure that Olivia's answer would be yes whether the question came with jewelry or not."

"Well, sure, but I can't do it without a ring!"

"Why don't you try? Tonight. You'll see that I'm right."

"Abby I can't just-"

"Why? You are so happy, Trevor. When you came in that door you said you were so excited to finally find a major and a profession that you would be good at because you could now have a life with Olivia. Why not just ask her?"

"Because, Abby! It's a marriage proposal. You just can't decide to do it on a whim."

"But you didn't just decide. You've talked to me about this for weeks and I'm sure you were thinking about it before then. You said you wanted to figure out what to major in and how to make money SO THAT you could marry her. That is not what I call deciding on a whim."

Trevor thought about it for a moment. "Maybe I will. Why don't you and Carlos meet me on the back patio of the waffle house at six? I'll call Olivia and tell her to do the same. See you tonight, Abb. I have to go get some things ready."

Trevor ran to his dorm room as fast as he possibly could, smiling the entire way. He burst into the room where Carlos was doing some homework. He noticed the unusually large smile on his friend's face.

"What is it, amigo?" Carlos asked.

"Look, we're going to meet the girls at Benny's tonight. We'll be on the back patio. Carlos I'm going to propose." Trevor was running frantically around the room, grabbing this and that.

"What?" Carlos asked, following Trevor with his gaze.

"And I-I don't have a ring, but I don't think you need a ring to ask a question do you?"

"Well, no. I don't think so. Unless it is another strange American custom."

"I'll get one later. Carlos," he paused his searching to look at his friend, "I want to marry her."

Carlos stood up and put one hand on Trevor's shoulder, "Let's go get you married my friend!"

Trevor went to several different stores, all of which he wouldn't have been caught dead in if he weren't proposing. Finally, he went to the back patio of Benny's waffle house and began decorating. The sun was beginning to set a little, making it harder and harder to see as the minutes went by. Finally, he was finished. His outside, proposal paradise was perfect. Now, all he and Carlos had to do was wait for the girls. They sat down in two of the four chairs they had carried out. That's when it began raining. It was only a light rain. Until it wasn't.

"Amigo! I have never seen so much rain in Colorado!" Carlos said, squinting while holding his jacket over his head.

"It's just a sprinkle!" Trevor said, trying to be louder than the rain pounding on the objects surrounding him.

Finally, the girls arrived. The string lights that Trevor had hung were beginning to sag. The daisies he had picked out were wilting from the weight of the water. The table cloths were collecting several puddles, and the food that Trevor had set out was ruined. He ran over and grabbed Olivia's hand. He was yelling, trying to be heard over the rain.

"I HAD THIS DECORATED PERFECTLY FOR YOU OLIVIA!"

"WHY? IT AIN'T MY BIRTHDAY IS IT!"

"NO! YOU SEE, I'M GOING TO BECOME A MECHANIC! THAT'S WHAT I WANT TO DO WITH MY LIFE! I FINALLY FIGURED IT OUT!"

"THAT'S WONDERFUL BABY! BUT WHAT DOES THAT HAVE TO DO WITH THE DEAD FLOWERS?"

"WELL, NOW I HAVE A WAY TO PROVIDE FOR A FAMILY. I HAVE A WAY TO PROVIDE FOR YOU." Trevor looked at the now soaked concrete, deciding if he wanted to get his trousers muddy. He decided he would. "I DON'T HAVE MONEY OR A RING. I DON'T HAVE A CLUE WHERE MY LIFE IS GOING. THE ONLY THING I DO HAVE THAT I KNOW WILL ALWAYS BE THERE IS YOU! OLIVIA, DO YOU WANT TO GET MARRIED?"

"WHAT? I CAN'T HEAR YOU OVER THE RAIN!"

"DID HE PROPOSE YET?" Abby asked Carlos.

"I DO NOT KNOW, SENORITA! I CANNOT HEAR A THING!"

"**WILL YOU MARRY ME?**" Trevor yelled even louder.

"WHAT?" Olivia asked.

Trevor stood up, smiling about how ridiculous he must look. "MARRY ME, WOMAN!"

"SERIOUSLY?" Olivia asked, with a growing smile on her face.

"I WOULDN'T BE YELLING IN THE RAIN, MAKING A FOOL OF MYSELF, WITH A BUNCH OF DEAD FLOWERS AROUND ME IF I WASN'T SERIOUS!"

"TREVOR, I LOVE YOU, BUT I'M AFRAID I CAN'T RIGHT NOW!"

"What?"

Eight

The Ferris Wheel

11/13/1978

Dear William,

Yes, my first date with Katherine was a success. In fact, I just got back from the second one. I mean, it only took Katherine almost a month of me hinting around that I liked her for her to realize what was going on. Or at least to agree to it. I mean, I was pulling out all the stops. I was at my smoothest when I was around her. She had to want to date me at some point, right?

Well, it worked. It worked like a CHARM!

Today, we went on a Ferris wheel. It was so much fun! I can't believe that I had never gone to one before! I felt like I could see the whole world from up there. Oh, it was amazing. She was amazing, Will. I was so nervous. I hope she couldn't tell. We were pointing out different things and having a great time. Finally, she said,

"Look, I had a-let's just say-weird childhood. I have not really been on many dates at all and, quite frankly, I like you. I've never said anything like this to a boy before, but I do. I really really would like this to go well."

"Really? You like me?" I asked with a mix of surprise and happiness in my voice.

"Well, don't you like me? Isn't that why we're here, doing this?"

"Uh-well, yeah. Yes, I do."

She smiled and looked down. "Good," she said.

"I think so."

We fidgeted a little, smiling, and went back to looking out at the incredible scenery around us. It was, as I said, amazing.

So, anyway, I got back from the Ferris wheel, and Fred, Anderson, and a couple of the other guys greeted me at the door standing in a line with their arms around each other singing,

"FOR HE'S A JOLLY GOOD FELLOW, FOR HE'S A JOLLY GOOD FELLOW, FOR HE'S A JOLLY GOOD FEL-LOOOOOOW! HE'S GOT BROWN!" (Brown is Katherine's last name.)

They started shooting questions at me, wanting to know every little thing that was said and done.

"Wow, Sanders, Brown said yes again! I think she's doomed,"

one guy said.

"You kissed her yet, Sanders?" Anderson asked.

"Nah," I said, "I'm laying low for a while. Don't want to scare someone like her off!" I said giving him a high five.

"You know, boys I think he likes her better than us!" Fred said as he reached for a high five.

"Don't be a fool, Fred! I wouldn't dare!" I said, laughing.

"How long do you think this one will last?" Anderson asked.

"I don't know," I said, a bit more seriously, "Kat's different. I really like her."

"OOOOOOOOO!" they all said together.

"Wow, real maturity, guys," I said.

"So, who are you going to choose for the best man at the wedding?" Fred asked.

"Pick me, Sanders!"

"No, pick me!"

"No, me!" they said, getting on their knees.

"Hey, you guys don't have to start fighting about that yet," I said,

"But, I don't know, give it a little time, we may have to draw a name from a hat."

"Yeah, we will!" Fred said.

So, enough about my sappy romance. I guess you're wondering what job I do here. Well, I'm in communications. Basically, I intercept messages and codes through the radio. It's some really interesting stuff. I also have a screen with information on it, talking about things that are happening around the world. So basically, I am productively watching tv and listening to the radio all day.

The guys and I play a lot of different games after lunch. We play softball, and handball, football, we box quite a bit too. It's a lot of fun. It's nice to have people close to you when you work. It helps you to have a good time in a place where maybe you wouldn't have as much fun.

Truth is Will, I didn't know if this was the right thing for me. It wasn't like the line between right and wrong was crystal clear because for some the army is the right choice. Honestly, I thought my family would be upset with me. I thought my actions could look like I was "leaving the family" as some would say.

Lately, I've been thinking. I've learned a lot, I've met some really incredible people, and none of that would have happened if I hadn't joined the army. Maybe, what's right for me is simply something different than what is right for other people. Maybe I was not leaving you and dad and mom; maybe I was chasing something that I wanted. Or, better yet, needed.

I just want you to know that I am always there for you and the rest of the family. I will come running or driving or swimming or surfing or flying or riding some sort of animal at a moment's notice. Lately, I've been learning how to operate a tank, so I could use that to get to you!

I guess, what I'm trying to say is, just because I'm going somewhere, doing something, being someone different than you might've thought I would be, that won't ever change the fact that I'm still your brother.

Anyways, enough talk about feelings. I was saying that I had all those pots and pans to wash in my last letter. Well, today, the chefs decided to have macaroni and cheese. That stuff is a nightmare to wash! If I have kids someday, we are never eating macaroni and cheese as a family. Anderson is also on kitchen duty. It's given me a chance to get to know him a little more, so that's been nice. I mean, we're not best friends or anything, but he is a pretty fun guy.

We talk about physical training and about old times in basic. He thinks it's just hilarious that I accidentally gave my drill sergeant a black eye.

I think, if you have just a few good people next to you, it makes this disastrous, broken, confusing, perfection-seeking, decision filled walk through life worth it. When you have people with you who see you for who you are, maybe even for who you never thought you could be, you are lifted up so much higher. You see things differently. You find beauty in the brokenness. You find happiness in confusion.

I know that I've only been on a few dates little brother, but I think Kat is it. Katherine makes me happy. Katherine makes it worthwhile. Fred and Anderson and everybody is helping me with all the in-between stuff of course. They're crazy.

Good lord, I just can't stop with the feelings tonight Will! I'm sorry to bore you. I hope you're having a good time in high

school. I will see you soon.
    Your brother,
    Ron Sanders

Nine

Definitely Maybe

Trevor blinked a few times, just to make sure he wasn't dreaming. He swallowed hard and slowly moved his mouth but no words were coming out. There he was. Standing in the rain, soaking wet, his almost fiancé standing before him. How could she do this to him? She didn't seem disappointed or sad or hesitant to hurt him or anything! How could a few simple words cause so much pain in so little time? She had only said them a few seconds prior, but it seemed like forty years before she said her next statement.

"Trevor? Trev, are you ok?" the words seemed to mix with the beat of the rain.

"Is it because I didn't have a ring? I knew I should've bought the ring first. The only reason I didn't was because Abby said-"

"Look," Olivia interrupted, "I made a promise to my daddy long ago that I would let the man of my choice ask for his blessin' before askin' for my hand. I don't plan on breakin' my promise to him."

"What?" Trevor asked, the hope slowly coming back.

"If you can ask for the blessin' of my father, I will, without a doubt, say yes to you."

Carlos and Abby stood next to the couple, leaning forward to hear the conversation over the rain.

"So, what you're saying is, not a yes, but not a no. It's definitely, maybe?"

Olivia put her eyebrows in a confused position. "I guess so."

Trevor looked from Olivia to Carlos, to Abby, and back to Olivia. He paused before saying, "Guys, we're going to Texas. Again."

"Trevor! We can't just ditch school!" Abby said.

"Amigo, I have muchos meetings at the shop in a couple of days. I cannot leave!" Carlos chimed in.

"We'll be back by then! Come on, is a couple of days of going to classes that you'll be attending for the next six months more important than my whole life?"

"Well, no bu-"

"Look, Olivia is who I want to spend the rest of my life with. If I need to go to the backside of the moon to ask her father for permission to marry her, then I'm going to. And I want my family there when I do. Now get packing."

Trevor raced back to his dorm room with Carlos on his tail. He didn't care if this night was a disaster. He wasn't going to think about it. Olivia gave him a definitely maybe and it was good enough for him. He just had to get past the father.

'I can do this,' he thought to himself, 'I can do this. I'm a nice guy. I've treated his daughter well. There is absolutely no problem here.'

But he couldn't think about that now. He had packing to do. He grabbed a few pieces of clothes and shoved them sloppily into his sad, broken, little cloth duffle bag. He decided to grab some letters and maybe catch up on some reading. He grabbed a few from the year his grandparents had been married, hoping to find some guidance for what to do or say to make it go a little better than it did earlier.

It was already dark outside, but that wasn't stopping Trevor. The four showed up at Carlos' truck about ten minutes later, bags in hand. Trevor asked Olivia to call her parents and ask if they could stay at their house. Naturally, Mr. and Mrs. Allen were completely fine with it. The group would be driving through the night so Olivia's parents put a key under the doormat, knowing they would be in before they woke up.

Trevor was in the passenger seat beside Carlos. About half an hour had passed since they had started the journey. It was only ten o'clock, but it seemed like it should be two in the morning. He looked over his shoulder, seeing Abby asleep with the side of her head pressed against the cold glass window. He looked to the left and saw Olivia sleeping with her blanket up to her neck. She was always cold. Trevor knew that. Why was he so happy he knew that?

He continued to look at her while he asked Carlos, "Why am I doing this?"

Carlos smiled. "I think you know, amigo."

"Why'd you say it like that?"

"You are doing this because your 'sweetheart', as she would say, wants to. Because you want to be a good husband for her."

"This whole 'ask the father' thing makes absolutely no sense to me. It's a completely useless and ridiculous thing."

"Well, maybe you should not be the one deciding that because you have such a rough relationship with your father."

Trevor put his head in his hands, wanting to say nothing and something at the same time. "I don't know, man. Maybe it's the never there thing, maybe it's the feeling that I've let him down every time I'm around him. It's like I was destined to be a disappointment to him or something. Did I ever tell you he just randomly shows up and tells me what I'm doing wrong in my life? Lots and lots of yelling. It's awful Carlos. And I don't think he's ever told me he loves me. I may have told him once. Maybe. I just can't seem to be in the same room with the guy."

"I know, amigo. So, that brings us back to the original question. Why are you doing this for Olivia? Why are you going to ask her father if you don't even understand the reason?"

Hearing her name, Olivia woke up. She began going back to sleep but put a pause on the ritual when she heard what was said next. Trevor's phone began vibrating. He already knew it was his father. He ignored it.

"Because I want to get married. I want to be a dad. I want her dad to like me…I want…I want her to love me."

Olivia smiled, adjusted the covers, and went back to sleep.

Carlos looked forward, driving with a smile on his face."You know, Abby told me about that conversation you had with her. About not knowing what your dream was. About not knowing how to dream."

Trevor looked down. "Yeah, I was just confused. I didn't know what I was saying. I was-"

"This situation we are in right now. You told us all to get packed el momento Olivia said there was a way for you to be with her. And here we are, driving through the night to get to Texas to ask a man, who you do not know very well, a simple question. Working as hard as you can to get something excelente. Someone excelente. Amigo, this scene, these people, that young lady sitting right behind me. Is this your dream?"

Ten

The Question We've All Been Waiting For

4/25/1979

To lieutenant Ron Sanders,

Due to your excellent performance in the department of communications, we have decided to use you for the good of our country. We have had several openings in our base in Turkey and, in the words of Uncle Sam, we need you. On October fifth, nineteen hundred seventy-nine, you will fly to and will land on the U.S. Army base in Turkey.

You will be on the third floor with approximately thirty other soldiers working in communications with you. If you do well, we will be stationing you in many other places. We've actually got a base in Germany that you can think about if this project goes smoothly.

We have been watching you for a while now and we believe

that you are our best man for the job. You have shown yourself to be incredible in both your physical tests and academic ones. The very complimentary letters that your sergeants have sent us on your behalf have hardly been ignored. We are well aware that this is your very first time being stationed anywhere, and that Turkey is not very close to where you are now. Not to worry soldier, you will get used to it. After all, this is what we trained you for.

If you learn anything from this business, it'll be that soldiers do not "put down roots". If you must be a plant, be a potted one because you will be moving around more than you ever have. You have been getting incredible word of mouth around here, Sanders and you seem extremely promising. Don't let us down.

Respectfully,
General Brewster

4/26/1979

Dear Katherine,

If Abigail did what I asked, you have found this letter on your bunk. You saw your name on it and thought 'Who would put a letter on my bed?' You sat down and opened the seal slowly and without ripping the envelope just like you always do. Just like you do with presents. Even if they're in wrapping paper. Yes, I know you. And you slowly took the letter out and carefully laid the envelope on your bed beside you.

Hello, Kat. It's Ronnie. And I love you so, let's get to the point.

Now I know that you just got back from dinner with me. If I didn't get nervous and change my mind, we took a walk through the cherry blossom lane that we walked through on our first date. I know you're probably thinking this is strange but just bear with me.

I am not very good at this sort of thing. I'm not great at knowing how to express my feelings for someone. I usually stand up in front of them and begin stuttering and saying um a lot and looking at my imperfectly tied shoelaces. I really wanted to get this one right, so I decided to write it. I've always been better at writing these things down, so here goes.

I got a letter last night from a General Brewster. I'm not sure who he is, but apparently, he's heard good things about me. They actually need someone to work at their communications base in Turkey. Well…Katherine, I ship out in October. I hate to leave you. I hate to leave at all. I want to be with you all the time but I'm afraid that's just not how it is going to happen. I guess this is what I get for being a potted plant. Sorry, that doesn't make any sense.

Anyways, we've been going out for a while now, Katherine, and as much as I dread leaving you, I took an oath, promising that I would. I took an oath to protect my country and my family. As much as I want to stay with you, Kat, I cannot betray that. But, there is a way for you to know that I love you and that I will always come back to you. Don't worry, I'll get there eventually. Just, hold on.

I got into this Army thing not knowing if this was the right choice. Not knowing anything really. For months upon months now I have been asking myself a question over and over and over again. How do I know if the decisions that I'm making are the right ones? How do I know that what I am doing is what God wants me to do?

Well, I have figured it out. At first, I thought it was the

approval of my parents. Joining the army was the first decision that I made as an adult. When you're a kid, the approval of your parents is your landmark. It's how you know if you did the right thing. While my parents were very supportive, I had this feeling in my stomach that this wasn't the answer.

Then I thought it had something to do with whether or not I could survive basic training. Now when you're in the moment, you're asking yourself that all the time. With the yelling and the marching and the waking up early enough to wake the chickens. I wasn't even sure if I'd survive. But you already knew that.

I love that we're both soldiers and can talk about this stuff with equal understanding! Sorry, off-topic. Don't worry Kat, I'll get there.

But this wasn't the answer either. I actually figured it out yesterday when the letter arrived. I chose the right path because I have been thriving. I am great at what I do, I have great friends, and I have you. My amazing, beautiful, funny, intelligent girlfriend whom I wouldn't trade for the world. I know I made the right choice because if I hadn't joined the army, I never would have met you. When you're with me it just seems like my life's on track. Wow, this is hard to say in a way that makes sense.

Anyway, that's what I want to talk to you about. I'm leaving in just a few months and I don't want to come back and not have you to come home to. I want to know that when I come home, you will be there waiting for me just the same as I will be waiting on the plane to get home to you.

Katherine Brown, I want to marry you. I've wanted to marry you for months but I thought proposing marriage to you on our first date might come across as "creepy". I want to marry you because when I'm with you I know I'm in the right place. I know that I made the right choice.

And look, I don't want you to think that I'm doing this on a whim. I've thought about this for a long time and I just cannot stand the thought of not coming home to you once I get off duty in Turkey. So, let's seal it, baby. Let's get married.

I know it sounds insane and you're probably thinking about all the ways something could go wrong but who cares! We love each other. We should get married. We should sign a paper saying we love each other. We should buy a little house to raise our kids in. Hey, if we still want to be soldiers once we're parents, we'll buy several little houses to raise our kids in. Just take a leap with me, Kat. Let's go sign some papers and kiss in front of some old guy holding a bible. Please?

Now you're thinking, 'But I don't know where you are my sweet, handsome, smart, adorable Ronnie! However, can we get married if I do not know where you are?' Hey, if you left out all the compliments, that's fine! We can work on complimenting each other as a love language some other time.

I am actually standing outside your window. If you go and look I'll wave to you. Do you see me? I'm smiling. I can promise that because I have been smiling the whole time I've been writing this letter. I've been smiling since I met you.

But WAIT! Stay seated! Calm down! Don't come running to me just yet. Try to refrain. I know it's hard to just look over my classic handsomeness, but just try to keep reading.

And now you're thinking, 'But my incredibly muscular, brilliant, blue-eyed Ronnie, where shall we go to get married?'

Let's face it. If we're being honest, you're probably thinking 'You weirdo, I never use the word shall'....Fair enough.

I know of a little justice of the piece office just a few miles away. He can do the ceremony for us, it won't be that expensive.

Come with me, Katherine! It doesn't matter what you wear. We can stop and get you something on the way, you can wear what you have on now for all I care. I just want to go. I want to do it. I love you so much and I want to be with you for the rest of our lives. So, one last time, marry me, Katherine Brown. Do me the honor of coming home to you.

(Hopefully) your husband,

Ron Sanders

P.S. Now you can let loose and run to me if you want to. I'll be waiting.

* * *

This is to certify to all who may concern
   that *Ron Lee Sanders*
   and *Katherine Linn Brown*
   were united on this day
   the *26th* **of** *April* **in the year** *1979*
   by the power invested in *Eugene B. Fernsby*
   and was witnessed and celebrated by *Susan J. Fernsby*
   Congratulations Mr. and Mrs. Ron Sanders!

Eleven

Green Eggs and Cinnamon Rolls

I t was six o'clock the next morning when the group arrived. Mr. Allen was already on his way to work; Mrs. Allen was still in bed. Carlos and Abby grabbed their bags from the truck bed and tiptoed inside. Trevor helped Olivia out of the truck and helped her with her bag. He gently grabbed her arm and stopped her outside of the house.

"What's wrong?" she asked.

Trevor rubbed his forehead as if debating if he should say what was on his mind. "Olivia, you know that I love you right?"

"Well, yeah."

"Because I wouldn't be doing this for someone I had no feelings for."

"What?"

"This thing with your dad. I wouldn't be driving for hours to ask a question like this to my girlfriend's dad," he paused, breathed, and finally decided to finish what he started, "if I had no feelings for her. Look, I have an awful relationship with my father. He just doesn't seem to like me that much. He doesn't want to be around me. I just don't know what it's like to have a father who actually cares what you do. I'm trying to say this as politely as possible."

"Say what, baby?"

"Well…why? Why is it so important for me to ask for your father's permission? I mean, I will gladly do it. I just wonder why?"

Olivia smiled and shifted her position. She brought Trevor to a bench on her front porch, sat down, and patted the space beside her. He sat too.

"I reckon I was in…first grade. Yeah, first grade. I went to class and sat down on the little rug on the floor while my teacher sat in a chair in front of me and the other kids.

"She opened a book sayin', 'The next three days for storytime, I'll be readin' *Green Eggs and Ham* by Dr. Seuss.'

"She read the first third of the book and I was in awe of its characters and the little rhymes. The book was so funny and the pictures were fascinatin'. But what I was really wonderin' about were those green eggs. Were they real? Did they taste good?

"At the end of storytime, I raised my hand and asked, 'Ms. Harper, are green eggs real?'

"She looked down at me and smiled like she was sayin' I had so much to learn.

"'No, Olivia,' she said. 'Green eggs are fake. Dr. Seuss made them up for his story and that is all they are: make-believe.'

"Well, I was disappointed. The green eggs in the picture looked so weird and sorta funny. But, of course, nothin' so funny lookin' and colorful could be outside of stories. That afternoon, I went home to my parents and told them all about Ms. Harper's book she had read. I told them that green eggs weren't real. That spared them the embarrassment of askin' the same question I had.

"'Olivia, green eggs are real,' daddy said.

"'No they're not! Ms. Harper said they're not!'

"Daddy smiled and said, 'But they are Olivia. I have a friend who has chickens that lay green eggs.'

"'Really?' I asked, excited.

"He does. I bet we could get some if we asked. You could show Ms. Harper your green eggs on Monday.'

"'I can?'

"'Of course. I'll call my friend and we can go to his farm and find you some green eggs.'

"So, when Monday rolled around, I brought a carton full of different colored eggs to school. There were blue ones and brown ones and pink ones. But what I was proudest of was the green ones.

"I sat the carton on her desk and said, 'Look, Ms. Harper! Green eggs are real! And blue ones, and pink ones too!'

"'Olivia,' she said, sorta skeptic like, 'did you color these eggs?'

"'No, Ms. Harper,' I said. 'My daddy found green eggs. Now you can eat green eggs and ham just like Sam I Am from the story!'

"I don't know if he knows this, but when I showed Ms. Harper my green eggs, my father went from daddy to hero. I was walkin' on the moon that day."

"Oh gosh, Olivia," Trevor said with a chuckle, trying not to reveal how much her story meant to him. " I can't believe he did that for you."

"Oh, it wasn't just that. It was everything. Everything my parents did was for one purpose: givin' me the opportunity to see the wonders of the world."

"Hence the eggs."

"Yep. Green eggs might not sound like a wonder to you, but they were to me, so my daddy found them. So I want to keep my promise to daddy because of all the times he gave me a reason to. And that's why I wanted you to ask his permission before you go askin' me. Is that ok?"

"It's perfect."

Trevor smiled before giving his girlfriend a hug. He had no explanation for it but seeing how much Olivia loved her father somehow made Trevor love her more. He opened his eyes, while still hugging her, and saw Carlos, Abby, and Mrs. Allen's squished faces against the window listening to everything. He laughed and let Olivia go. Then he looked around, noticing something.

"Hey, this is exactly where I asked you to go on our first date last year! Do you remember that?"

"Oh yeah! That was when momma was sick and you took me down here to visit her. How many times are you gonna do this Trevor?" she asked, smiling.

"As many times as you need me to," he answered.

They went inside. Mrs. Allen gave Olivia a hug as they caught up with each other in about two minutes. Then she helped Trevor with the bags and gave him a one-armed hug while she said how good it was to see him. The group put their bags in the designated rooms that they had slept in the last time. Mrs. Allen asked if anyone wanted any cinnamon rolls and started unwrapping the tube when the answer was affirmative.

"Can I help you with anything ma'am?" Trevor asked when they were both in the kitchen.

"Of course!" She said as she split the cold, uncooked cinnamon rolls into two equal portions. "It's really great to see all of you here. What's the occasion? Are you visiting some friends?"

"No," Trevor said, focusing deeply on his cinnamon rolls, "I actually had a question for Mr. Allen."

"Oh, you didn't have to come all the way down here. You could've called him you know. He wouldn't have minded."

"I know," he said, still looking at the cinnamon rolls, "but I just really wanted to ask this one in person."

"Well, ok, what's the question? Is it something I can help you with?"

"I actually came down here," Trevor decided to be a man and look up at her, "I came down here to ask Mr. Allen for Olivia's hand…in-in marriage."

"You did?" Mrs. Allen said with a smile slowly spreading from ear to ear. "Does Olivia know?"

"Yes ma'am. She asked me if I would ask her dad before I asked her…I hope you know I love your daughter Mrs. Allen. I'd do anything for her. You-uh-you did a really good job."

Mrs. Allen smiled and put her hand on her chest. "Well, thank you, Mr. Foster. You are so kind. May I just say one thing?"

"Sure."

"I'm glad it was you."

Twelve

Wool Socks

10/4/1979

Dear Katherine,

I arrived in Turkey four days ago. I'm sorry it took me a few days to write, but I have been a little busy and you'll soon see why. To answer the question in your last letter, it's pretty hot here. It's in the seventies and eighties mostly, but you know how I love warm weather.

So let me start by telling you the reason I haven't written. And believe me, it is a real story. I'm not just making this up. We were supposed to receive our uniforms upon arrival. I walked around the base until I spotted the barracks. I went up the stairs until I got to floor number three and finally found my bunk and sat my bag on top of it. I walked back down to the first floor which was full of offices. I had no idea which person to talk to for receiving my uniform. I asked around a little and finally, a lady pointed to a Colonel around forty years of age sitting at a desk.

He was reading some files and seemed really focused. I stood in attention and waited for him to address me so that I could ask him the question. I don't know if he couldn't see well, was lost in thought, or just ignored me, but he didn't look up from his papers for several minutes. I cleared my throat, in an attempt to be noticed and not be disrespectful. He looked up, then at the name tag that was dangling around my neck.

"Sanders huh," he said looking back at the papers on his desk.

"Yes sir. I'm with the new communication soldiers."

"Of course you are, because you're new here and way too young for your job and know nothing about what is going on," he said (kind of condescendingly).

"Um, I don't know sir, I've been at this for over a year now, not counting basic. I know something about the ways of the Army," Colonel Moore looked at me over his glasses. I coughed and straightened my posture before I said, "I was just wondering where I could get my uniform?"

"Down the hall, first door on the right, Sanders."

"Thank you," I said, pausing to read the name on his desk, "Colonel Moore."

I started walking away when he yelled behind me in a phony country accent, "If you get promoted to 'Colonel Sanders' will you make me some of that good Kentucky fried chicken? Or will you go big and open up your own fast food restaurant?"

The whole floor erupted with laughter. My face turned bright red and I paused in my steps. I closed my eyes and breathed, trying to drown the sound of the laughing out. I opened my eyes, the red in my cheeks slowly fading away, and I started walking towards the door I was instructed to find.

'I'm not here to fight with a Colonel, I'm here to get my uniform,' I kept telling myself.

As I kept walking, without looking back, I thought about how rude that man had been. I was honestly glad that our conversation was over and hoped a similar one would never happen again. Ok, let me rephrase that, I would do ANYTHING to see that a similar conversation with Colonel Moore never happens again.

I found the door he had described and went inside. I was given two uniforms, one for work and the other for formal events, pictures, and dinners and things. I thanked the man who had found them for me and started back towards the stairs.

I went to the locker next to my bunk to hang up my formal uniform and to change into my work uniform. The uniform I have here in Turkey is so much better than the one I was given in the states. I guess they knew it would be hot here because the uniform kept me cool the whole day. I was given socks that had the Army's logo on the top. They felt a bit different from the ones in America. I couldn't quite put my finger on it.

Well anyways, I was going about my day and my feet and my legs began itching terribly. I thought maybe it was just the heat or something. I pulled my pant leg up a bit to see what was causing the itching and I saw little red dots all over my legs. I had no idea what was going on.

As the day went on, the bumps began growing in size and in itchiness. My legs began sweating as the little rashes continued to grow. I decided to take a shower in case I had gotten into some sort of poison ivy or something. That didn't help.

Well, after a while, it became harder and harder to walk. This was after my throat seemed to close and kept me from breathing. So I was limping, itching, gasping, and sweating. Not exactly the healthiest of combinations.

Around the end of the day, the itching had become unbearable and my feet were throbbing. I went to my bunk and took my boots off, still struggling to breathe. Kat, my feet were swollen to around three times the size. I wondered, not for the first time, what it could be. Finally, I thought of something. Maybe it was the socks!

I went downstairs, making pain-filled faces or biting my tongue every time my feet hit the ground. I limped my way to the same room where I had received my uniform and knocked on the open door. A man was filing papers and turned around when he heard me. It was Colonel Moore.

"I apologize for interrupting you...sir" I said, trying with everything in me to not shout with pain as my feet were throbbing and itching worse and worse, "but what are the socks given with the uniform made out of?"

He rolled his eyes, "Wool, moran. You really are new here aren't you?"

"Yep, new. Really new," I said. I WANTED to say something about all the weapons I have learned how to use or how great at hand to hand combat I have become. I decided to refrain. "Do you know where a hospital might be?" I asked.

"What would *you* need a hospital for? Are you not smart enough to find one of the largest buildings on the base all by your little self Sanders?"

"You don't ha-" I started to say something I would have regretted so I just bit my tongue before I said, "Thank you for your time, Colonel."

So, back to the wool socks. Yes, you remembered correctly, Kat, I am SEVERELY allergic to wool. I asked around and finally found a hospital. I wanted them to just give me a pill or some ointment or something, but they decided to hold me in the hospital for a night. So, I spent my first night in Turkey in a hospital. It wasn't exactly the first impression I was trying to make.

Anyway, I've been out of the hospital for the past couple of nights. Work has gone really well, except for Colonel Moore. He is just so rude! He keeps saying awfully mean things. This situation is very odd because the guy is the authority. If he was just a lieutenant like me, I would've already fought him or reported him or something. But with Colonel Moore, who am I going to report him to? Himself?

It's as if he knows that I'm going to mess up. Like I have no hope of being anything but an inexperienced new guy. I'd just like to give him a piece of my mind.

As of right now, I am just trying to be sensible, polite, and professional with him. Who knows, maybe somebody higher up than me will notice how nice I have been to him and give me a promotion or something. This all sounds really corny. I know it sounds like I'm just signing up to get pushed around, but it just isn't true. Colonel Moore is the authority and, even though he hasn't done anything to deserve my respect, that's exactly what I'm going to give him. I mean, I have to give him some credit for serving his country and getting promoted to Colonel.

I've been reading about bullies in the bible (proud of me aren't you Kat) and I found a verse: If your enemy is hungry, give him bread to eat, and if he is thirsty, give him water to drink. In doing this, you will heap burning coals on his head, and the LORD will reward you.-Proverbs 25:21. So, my being respectful to Colonel Moore is the equivalent of giving him water to drink. And then there's that part at the end that says the Lord will reward me for it. Not that that's what I'm working towards, it just helps me to know if I'm doing the right thing.

Anyway, they haven't given me a date when I can come back to the states and see you again. I miss you so very much. I want to come home so badly, and yet I want to stay. Next time, you are definitely coming with me. I love you, Katherine Sanders.

Your husband,

Ronnie

Mr. Allen's Breakfast

Trevor closed the letter and placed it back into the envelope. He was blown away by how much Colonel Moore from his Grandpa's letter reminded him of his father. Maybe that scripture that he had mentioned would help Trevor's situation. Proverbs 25:21: If your enemy is hungry, give him bread to eat, and if he is thirsty, give him water to drink. If Ronnie's symbolic water to Colonel Moore was being respectful, what was Trevor's for his father?

He looked at his watch. Seven o'clock. He had to go to breakfast with the father of his girlfriend today. Yikes. He got out of bed and put his feet on the carpet. Carlos moved a little on his blow-up mattress on the floor. Trevor was careful not to wake him as he headed for the door.

In the hall, Trevor saw his cousin with her back towards him as she slowly closed the door to her and Olivia's room. She turned around and jumped a little when she saw Trevor.

"What are you doing up?" he whispered through a laugh.

"I always get up at seven. What's your excuse?"

"I thought I'd start getting ready to leave."

"Oh right, breakfast with the father-in-law."

"Yeah," Trevor said nervously.

"Well, I'll be in the living room if you need anything."

"Ok, Abb."

Trevor tiptoed across the hall to the bathroom. He was careful to make sure he looked presentable for his father-in-law. He collected the keys to Carlos' truck and tiptoed to the living room where Abby sat on the grey sectional couch reading a book.

"How do I look?" Trevor asked.

Abby put her book down and removed her reading glasses. "Turn around," she said, moving her hand in a circular motion.

"What? No!"

"Why?" she asked with a smile on her face, suggesting she knew the answer.

"Because then you're going to bring up that story!"

"What story?" she asked, the smile still growing.

"That story about when we were little and all the other cousins were at the grandparent's house."

"And you and the rest of the boys…" Abby said, setting the scene for Trevor to finish the story.

"And we…"

"Go on," she said, mischievously.

"We took the dress up scarves and necklaces that Grandma had gotten for you and gave you a fashion show."

Abby erupted with laughter as she fell back on the couch. "You had it down to the feathers and sunglasses!"

"I was like six or something, ok?" he said, trying to remain mad as a smile crept onto his face.

"And you were walking up and down the porch in your ridiculous 'model walk'"

"Would you just shut up?"

"Aw, I'm sorry," Abby said, getting up to hug him.

"No you're not," Trevor shot back trying, and failing, not to laugh.

"No, I'm not," she said, laughing as her arms went around his neck. "Do you remember why you guys did that?"

"What? No."

"I had just fallen off of that rock wall right next to the driveway. My knees and elbows were bleeding. You guys tried to help me feel better."

"Did it help?"

Abby smiled for a moment. "You know, you definitely looked better then than you do now."

"Gee thanks, Abb. Right before talking to the father-in-law."

She laughed before she said, "You look great."

"Thanks."

"I mean, you'd look better with a feathered scarf around your neck, but that's just me."

"Oh look at the time," Trevor said.

He double-checked to make sure he had everything he needed before he left. He had been given permission from Carlos to use his truck the day before. Using that, Trevor made it to the cafe where he was meeting Mr. Allen.

"The Country Cafe" was the name on the glass door that Trevor had entered. The place was full of windows and colorful chairs and tables. It had a perfect view of a lake through the back window of the restaurant. He began walking forward towards the table that Mr. Allen was sitting at.

He wore a blue, button-down shirt that was tucked into his worn-out jeans. He had glasses and a full head of curly grey hair, with the occasional black in it. When Trevor was within two feet of the table, Mr. Allen stood up and offered his hand.

"Trevor! It's so nice to see you again!" he said, shaking his hand.

"Absolutely. You as well."

"Would you like a menu?"

"Oh, yes sir. Please."

Mr. Allen waved a waitress over and asked for a breakfast menu. Trevor nervously sat through small talk about the drive over and the eggs and sausage he was eating. They talked of the weather and of school. Finally, Mr. Allen had asked the question that Trevor had been both dreading and anticipating.

"So, Trevor, what-uh-was there a reason you were wanting to have breakfast with me?"

He adjusted a bit in his seat and answered, "Actually, there was. I had a question for you. A big one. One that will affect both you and me."

"Oh wow. Well, you've got my attention."

"Yeah. So-well-before I start I would just like you to know that I am studying to become a mechanic. I've already got a job offer. They're just waiting for me to get done with school. It's a busy little shop. It would be a steady paycheck. Enough to keep some lights on."

"Well, I think that's wonderful. Mechanics are extremely underappreciated these days for what all they do."

"Yeah. So anyway, now that I've got a job, I want to start a family."

Mr. Allen coughed; looked down, then back up again. He rubbed both of his legs with his hands and said, "Uh-huh."

"I want to start a family with your daughter."

"Mhmm" Mr. Allen answered as he rubbed his eyelids.

"I love her very much, Mr. Allen, and I didn't even want to ask her to marry me until I was completely sure I had a way to provide for her. Actually, I asked her already. She said she couldn't say yes unless you accepted me as part of your family," That statement seemed to catch Mr. Allen off guard. His eyes widened as he suddenly began to look proud. "You did a great job with her, Mr. Allen. She loves you very much. Look, she'll always be your little girl, and unless you say yes to the question coming up, she will never want to be my wife. I just want you to know how happy she makes me feel. It's like I'm a completely different person," Trevor paused and thought about what to say next. "You know, that quote 'Yesterday is history; tomorrow a mystery; but today is a gift'?"

"Yes."

"Well, since I was little, my grandma had that quote on her fridge. That 'tomorrow a mystery' part always seemed to scare me. I grew up in a place where if you didn't know what was coming, you better prepare for the worst. I was taught that people were out to get me, and some of them really were. Mysteries were bad things that we should steer away from. But when I'm with Olivia, 'tomorrow a mystery' sounds like fun. It reminds me of all the spectacular possibilities coming for me. She makes me happy and…and…well I can't think of the right adjectives for what I'm trying to describe. All I know is that I love her and in order for my life to go anywhere, she has to be with me. She has to support me and keep me grounded and make me who I am. She accepts me as I am, but at the same time, she influences the person I'm becoming. So, after hearing all of that, here comes the question we've all been waiting for. Please Mr. Allen, please let me marry your daughter, Olivia, because I promise that no-one will ever love her more than I do. Please, sir. Please."

Mr. Allen stood up and straightened his shirt. Trevor immediately started having a miniature argument in his brain about whether Mr. Allen was getting ready to punch him or hug him. Mr. Allen stretched out his hand, offering to help Trevor stand. When he got to his feet, Mr. Allen wrapped both his hands around the hand of the man who was about to be his son-in-law.

"You can absolutely marry my daughter. Nothing makes me happier than to see how happy she is with you. I would be honored to call you my son."

Trevor had never felt so happy or accomplished or…right than he did at that exact moment. It was a feeling that he had never quite had before. He wished he could freeze the moment, the feeling.

Trevor drove back to the Allens' house to share the good news. He was unable to wipe the smile off of his face. He felt that nothing would. Until something did. Someone did. He pulled the truck into the driveway. He saw someone standing on the porch about to knock on the door.

"Dad?"

Fourteen

"SHE'S PREGNANT, FRED"

10/10/1979

My Katherine,

I miss you also. More than you know. I am beyond excited about our baby! Do not be afraid of what is going to happen in the future. I will be home very soon, Kat. I will not miss the birth of our child. I can't wait to wrap my arms around you two! I read the part about you wanting to quit the army. If that is what you are wanting to do, I support it for I support you. Maybe, if I'm called out of the country again, and you are not serving anymore, you can come with me! I miss you so very much, Katherine. I am more than happy about the baby!

Your husband,

Ron

10/10/1979

FRED!

SHE'S PREGNANT! I'm going to be a father! I'm barely a husband! And no I don't want any inappropriate jokes from you when you write me back! I can't believe this! I don't know what to say! Or do! I'm losing my mind! I've been PACING for the last HOUR!

SHE'S PREGNANT FRED! I can't be a father! I'm a soldier! I have to travel for my job! Father's don't travel! Father's don't leave! They have no fun whatsoever! They stay in their little towns and….go bowling and…their wives get mad when they come home late! They get little apartments and befriend their landlords and sing songs to babies—YES I'M JUST DESCRIBING OLD SITCOMS!

I don't know how to be a father! I don't know anything! I was just getting used to being an adult, and then a soldier, and then a husband, and now a…FATHER? What do I do, Fred? You're my best friend! You're supposed to know this stuff!

I don't think I've ever even held a baby! When William was born I wasn't trusted to hold him. I was just a kid. I don't remember ever holding a baby! I don't know how to change diapers, or heat up milk bottles, or build cribs! And what if the baby is an insane toddler? I can't handle that, Fred!

And no I can't tell Katherine! She's got enough on her plate. She's the one who's going to be pushing a miniature human out of her body, not me.

Holy cow! How can I be so self-absorbed as to be worrying about me me me when Katherine is probably freaking out about giving birth? That's another reason why I can't take care of a child. Everything is always about me, me, me.

What if I'm a terrible example to a kid? I mean, I have a temper and I have to work a lot. I don't know what to do! I can barely see straight!

I bet every other soon-to-be-parent is constantly daydreaming about all the fun they'll have with their kid and about all the fun games they'll play and all the nights they'll rock them to sleep. NOT ME!

What do I do? What do I do? What do I do? Why am I so much more comfortable learning to drive tanks and finding encrypted messages at the risk of enemies running to catch the guy who ruined their plan? I'm CLUELESS!

Ok, ok, ok, all I need to do is find something to get my mind off of it. Think about work and and and morse code and and and uh… Colonel Moore! Wait, I forgot to write and tell you what he did a couple of days ago. That'll get my mind off of the situation!

I was at my computer the other day with my headphones on. I was writing down the codes I was receiving. Colonel Moore walked over to my desk and stood over my computer. I removed my headphones and looked up.

"Sanders, I'd like a word."

I took a huge gulp of air. "Sir?"

He gestured to me to follow him. We walked to the farther side of the room, out of the hearing length of the other soldiers. I braced myself to get ready to not yell at him when he made another rude comment about Colonel Sanders. I was providing water and food to the hungry and thirsty, just like Jesus had said. I was remaining calm. Unexpectedly, he placed his huge hand on my shoulder.

"You're a good soldier, Sanders."

I was in shock. I stood there, almost unable to move, just blinking. I tried to form words, but nothing was coming out of my mouth when it opened. He went on.

"Recently, a soldier, about your age, put me in my place. He was saying how much I was being a grouch about just, ridiculous things. He started saying how much he disliked the fact that I had been singling you out in particular. He went on about how much you deserve my respect because of all of the junk you have gone through because of me. And all the while, you kept calm and said nothing about it. He told me that he was your friend and that he would stand up for you. He told me that I should apologize to you," My mind froze there. Who could that be? I haven't had any time to talk to anybody really since I got here. "So, I'd just like to say that I am very sorry about making fun of your name and not thinking you could do your job properly. I was proven extremely wrong. You are good at what you do, soldier."

"Thank you for apologizing, sir. The gesture is highly appreciated." I paused. "Could you tell me who the soldier was who told you about me? I'm not trying to pry, but I just wonder who would do something like that for me."

"I understand. His name is Richard," he said.

"Richard?"

"Yes. Richard Anderson."

"Anderson? Anderson's here? I didn't know that!" I said, growing more and more excited.

"He's a chef."

"Really?"

"Yes."

"I'm sorry to be rude, Colonel Moore, but I have to go. May I be excused?"

"Absolutely," he said.

Then he saluted me. Me! He saluted me! I couldn't believe it. I got a salute from a Colonel. Of course, I couldn't think about that just then. I had a friend to find. I ran down the hall and took a left at the kitchen door. The kitchen was huge and there had to be at least twenty U.S. army chefs back there. I stood in the doorway and yelled,

"Is there a soldier named Anderson here?" he popped his head out from behind some of the chefs.

"Here."

I gestured my hand for him to come towards me. He did.

"I heard what you did for me, Anderson."

He rubbed the back of his neck while he said, "You don't think

I'll get fired for it, do you?"

"Not if Colonel Moore has anything to say about it."

"What?" he asked with both hope and confusion in his eyes.

"He apologized to me because of what you said to him. I think he actually likes you for yelling at him."

"He does?"

"I think so."

"Wow. I didn't even know Colonel Moore knew how to like something."

"Well, I think you just taught him how," I said. Anderson smiled. I could tell he was nervous. I think he was trying to avoid saying the wrong thing. "I just really wanted to thank you for what you did."

"Oh, that's ok. You deserved it."

There was a pause before I said, "So, you're a chef now? I could tell when we were washing dishes together way back when that you liked the kitchen."

"Yeah! I was studying to be a communications officer like you, but this is what I really like doing. Plus, I failed almost all of my classes."

I laughed. Probably shouldn't have done that. "Well, I don't know if I've eaten anything that you specifically have made, but everything I have eaten here has been good. I'm sure you're an excellent chef."

"Thanks, Sanders. I bet that you're great at your job too."

"Thanks. Well, I won't keep you from your work. Don't be a stranger, ok Anderson? We'll get some lunch sometime."

"That sounds good. I'm glad Colonel Moore is off of your back."

"Me too, buddy. Thanks again."

"Anytime."

I watched him through the window of the door. He started doing that dance he always does that looks like a chicken having a seizure while repeatedly saying "yes yes yes yes". He's such a funny guy. I just thought since he is your friend too that you might like to know that he's doing well.

Anyways, Fred, I heard you were stationed in Germany or something? Are you still in communications? Maybe one of these days we can work together again. You'll have to come to visit and meet my baby.

Oh yeah…she's having a baby.

Hopefully, I'll see you soon.

Your friend,

Ron Sanders

Fifteen

The Confrontation

*f your enemy is hungry, give him food to eat; if he is thirsty, give him water to drink. In doing this, you will heap burning coals on his head, and the LORD will reward you.-Proverbs 25: 21-22.

Trevor repeated that verse over and over while he got out of the green pick up truck. It was nine in the morning. Everybody should be awake by now. His father turned his head before his fist hit the door. Trevor walked towards him.

"What…what are you doing here dad?" he asked nervously.

"I can't see my son?"

'Give him water to drink Trevor. God will reward you,' he said in his head. "Can I help you with something?"

"Does your phone work, son?"

"Yes sir."

"Oh really? I wouldn't know. It goes to voicemail every time I call."

"I've been really busy, dad."

"Oh yeah?   I got one of those stupid schedules for your ridiculous college so that I wouldn't call you when you were in class. I thought, maybe, just maybe, he'll answer me this way. This way he won't have anything to do when I'm calling. What's the deal, Foster?"

"I-I-I…" Trevor couldn't say what he was thinking. He couldn't say that he didn't want his father to be disappointed in him. He couldn't say that was the reason he'd avoided his calls. It seemed like disappointing him was the only thing Trevor had done lately.

"Well?" Mr. Foster asked, arms crossed.

"How'd you know where I was, dad?"

"I called the phone the front desk guy has in your building. He told me you went to Texas. What are you doing in Texas, Trevor?"

That's when Olivia walked out. Trevor cringed. He wished she would've stayed inside. He didn't want her to see him this way.

"Who's this, baby?" she asked.

"BABY?" Mr. Foster asked, "Trevor, I demand to know just who this is."

Trevor sighed. "Olivia, this is my dad, Eric. Dad, this is Olivia. She-uh-we're…getting married soon."

"Oh great. That's just fantastic," Mr. Foster said sarcastically, "I'd love to talk about it over cupcakes and icecream but I'm a little busy right now! Can we get back to our conversation?"

"Dad, you asked."

"That has nothing to do with it."

"Olivia, why don't you go back inside," Trevor said, keeping eye contact with his father.

"Are you sure?"

"Yeah."

"Well, alright then. I reckon I'll go get a glass of water."

Trevor was reminded to repeat the verse again. 'Give him water to drink Trevor. Stay calm Trevor. God will reward you.'

"This isn't because I refused your calls, is it dad?"

"What? Of course it-"

"It's because I left the city to come to college. It's because I left you to be someone else. Someone you didn't raise."

"Don't be-"

"I just want you to know it wasn't your fault."

"What?"

"I love you, dad. I always have."

"Are you-"

"I love you I love you I love you. You could never do anything to make me think any differently. I'm sorry I didn't say it enough growing up. It is something I regret more than anything."

"Trev-"

"Dad, you have to understand something. I left because it was something I had to do, for myself. I left because I didn't like the person I was becoming-"

"You can't just-"

"I left because I didn't want to feel like I was disappointing you anymore."

"You-"

"And I want you to know I don't blame you for my struggling

as a kid. It was my fault. But it's in the past!"

"I don't-"

"Olivia!" Trevor yelled with a smile on his face, "Would you come out here please? Bring Abby and Carlos too!"

In a matter of seconds, his friends were all standing on the porch with him, facing his father. They all began asking questions but he interrupted them.

"Dad, these are my friends. You remember Abby and Carlos don't you?" he nodded. "This is who I am. They make me who I am. They inspire me and help me to become a better person than the boy you once knew, not the person you raised, but the person I became. I don't know if you knew this, but I always felt alone in the city. I felt like you were never there and I barely had any friends. None of which I trusted. Dad, I have a family because of these people. You can be a part of my family. Just because we're blood-related, you and I, doesn't mean we're family. It means we're relatives. It doesn't have to stay like this dad. I don't want it to." Trevor walked towards his father. "This is who I've become. I honestly believe this is who I'm supposed to be, and where. Would you like to be a part of this family, dad? All of us are different. Be different with us, dad. Please."

Mr. Foster thought for a bit. Finally, he inhaled a steadying breath and said, "You're getting married, huh?"

Trevor turned and put his hand towards Olivia. She grabbed it, walked forward, and Trevor turned back around smiling, "Sure am. I just asked for her father's blessing. He said we could go ahead."

"He did?" Olivia asked excitedly.

"Of course!"

"Congratulations guys!" Abby whispered from behind them.

"We should celebrate or somethin'," Olivia said.

"Yeah. We'll wait and throw a party or something tomorrow. That way Mr. Allen will be off of work early so he can be a part too," Trevor added.

Carlos stepped forward, "Would you like to come, señor Foster."

"You're welcome to sir," Abby added.

"We wouldn't have it no other way," Olivia added.

Trevor smiled with his friends around him. "What do you say, dad?"

"Oh I-I don't know. We'll see, kid. I have to go."

"We'll see you tomorrow then?" Trevor asked as Mr. Foster walked towards his car. He just smiled at them.

Abby stepped forward and stood next to her cousin. "Do you

think he'll come?" she asked.

"Probably not," Trevor answered. "All that matters is he knows I love him. It'd be nice if I knew he loved me."

"He'll come amigo," Carlos said as he grabbed his friend's shoulder.

"Sure he will!" Olivia added. "And when he does, you'll know just how much he loves you."

Sixteen

Virginian Opportunity

4/13/1980

Future Staff Sergeant Ron Sanders,

We received the request for being stationed in the United States again. We have an opening in our base in Virginia for a staff sergeant. You would no longer be working in communications but it would require your experience in the communication field.

You can take your position starting on July 2, 1980. If it were not for that recommendation from Colonel Moore, we would have just suggested taking some of your vacation days. But because of your wife's situation and the recommendation, we've decided on you for the position.

Within your new position, you will be dealing with new soldiers, just out of basic. You will be introducing them to the newly arrived technology we have received. This will require you to know the instruments backward and forwards before teaching. Keep in mind that you will be pressed to know the material.

You will be teaching them to learn morse code and to intercept messages from the radio. You will also teach them to find encoded messages on the television. You will be teaching two six-week-long courses in the span of twenty days. This will be a hard-pressed job and you may feel that you're being overworked. However, from what Colonel Moore has written to us about you, you seem to fit the bill perfectly.

Congratulations on the baby.

Respectfully,

General Brewster

4/27/1980

Dear Katherine,

I'm coming home! Or, to Virginia at least, at the beginning of July! It'll be right on time to see the baby! It worked out just perfectly! And you'll never guess who is to thank: Colonel Moore.

I got the letter from general Brewster, it's in the envelope with this one, and it said they accepted my request to move to America again. It said that it was all because of the fantastic recommendation that Colonel Moore gave me. I was confused because I never asked for a recommendation or a new position. I just thought I'd take a month or two off to help you and then return to Turkey.

As you know, for a new position to be requested I would've had to go to Colonel Moore's office, ask him to write to General Brewster, and request a station somewhere else. Well, all I remembered doing was telling him I was planning to take a couple of months off around July. I was pretty confused. So anyway, I went to his office and asked about it.

"Colonel Moore," I said, standing in attention, "may I speak with you, sir?"

"Of course, sit down. What is it?"

"Oh, nothing much. I just-uh-had a question that I thought you might be able to answer."

"What is it, boy?"

"Did you send a request for me to go back to America?"

"In our meeting last week, you said something about taking a couple of months to help your wife because she's expecting. I said I would try to find some sort of solution, and I did."

Oh, that Colonel Moore. Always being rudely nice. "But, if I may be so bold, why?" I asked.

"Well, you only get so many vacation days, and I thought your wife would be needing you more than you thought. Take it from a fellow father. I know what I'm talking about."

'Colonel Moore has a kid?' I thought.

"You don't have to change positions if you do not wish," he said. "It was only an idea."

"Oh no, sir! I would love to take it." I wondered if I should ask the question I really wanted to. After a moment, I did. "The letter I received from General Brewster said you had written a recommendation about me?"

Colonel Moore paused and leaned forward, as if waiting for me to say something else, "Oh. That was all? Yeah, yeah I did. Yep. That was me."

I nodded slowly as the awkward silence surrounded us. Colonel Moore was looking around his office as if thinking of redecorating. You could hear the soldiers marching outside. It was so quiet.

"Ok. Well, I should probably go then," I finally said.

Then we awkwardly started talking at the same time.

"Ok well, I'll see-"

"You have a good-"

"It was nice-"

"Thanks for sto-"

"See you tomor-"

"Mhmm-"

I walked out of the office and shut the door, then exhaled a breath of relief. I just couldn't believe he had done that for me! I guess this is what God meant about rewarding me for being kind to Colonel Moore. As much as I didn't want to respect him when I first got here; all those times I almost yelled at him or almost punched him or almost did to him what he deserved and yet didn't. That was me giving water to a thirsty person.

Then Anderson talked to him about me, Colonel Moore apologized to me, AND THEN found me a job near you, that was my reward. I'll tell you something, Kat, God keeps his promises. Even the ones He wrote thousands of years ago when the Bible was written.

Who knew that those promises were for me? When they were written, maybe they were for David or Moses or John the baptist, or all the other bible characters. Maybe the Bible's authors saw the word of God as their hope (and it was!) but today, right now, God's promises are for me. They're my hope. I know that you already knew this Kat, but I just needed to talk to someone about it.

And it's so awesome because years and years ago when it was David and Moses' hope, God knew that I would need it. That in 1980, a soldier from Indiana will need the verse Proverbs 25:21. I can't help but think that God told Solomon (he wrote Proverbs) to write down the twenty-first verse in the twenty-fifth chapter because he knew that I would need it.

I'm so happy, Kat! I can't wait to see you! It'll be sooner than you think. I can't wait to meet the baby!

Love,

Ronnie

Party Disappointment

The group decided that they would keep the guestlist for the celebration small. Olivia was growing more and more excited, which made Trevor happy. Mr. Allen would be there in a few hours. Mrs. Allen's aunt, who was also her next-door neighbor, was invited to their celebration. Olivia said she had been like another grandmother when her grandparents had passed.

The only other person was his dad. Trevor found himself hoping that his father would come. This was a feeling he was not used to. He had never wanted to be around his dad in the past because he reminded him of who he once was. As much as he was angry with him for doing that over the years, he loved him even more. Even if the man never said, "I love you".

Trevor went outside to begin heating up the grill. Carlos was behind him, holding hamburgers and hotdogs on a plate.

"The best thing that has come from your country is definitely hamburgers, amigo," Carlos said. "I am excited about this."

Trevor laughed, "I forgot about your obsession with hamburgers! Have you tried them with pickles?"

"Amigo, I have tried them with barbeque sauce, onions, pickles, hot sauce, mayonnaise, rice-"

"You put rice on a hamburger?" Trevor asked, turning knobs on the grill.

"Si! I have to stay true to my Cuban roots, amigo!"

"I've never heard of rice hamburgers from Cuba before, Carlos."

"No, but you will!"

He laughed again. "Help me cook this food, you hamburger addict."

The two put their favorite spices on the patties and closed the grill while waiting for them to cook through. They sat on a little bench the Allens had outside. When the conversation died down, Carlos asked a question,

"Do you think your father will come?"

"I honestly don't know Carlos. I wasn't thinking he would yesterday, but today, I don't know."

"Do you want him there?"

"I think so."

"Pero, when we were coming to Texas, you said you couldn't be in the same room with señor Foster."

"Well, that was before I talked to him. When I saw him outside yesterday I was just so mad. I was really really mad. I had a whole list of reasons. Then, I don't know, I told myself to speak kindly to him and suddenly, it was like all those reasons were being erased. I didn't see the guy I was mad at anymore. I saw my dad. The only one I have. I remembered that he's my father and he took care of me when he and mom got divorced. He did the best he could. I guess…I just thought…he deserved to know what I was thinking. You know?"

"You are a much better person than I, señor," Carlos answered, shaking his head as he placed the patties on the grill.

"Oh, I doubt that. I'm just trying to follow an example."

"Who's example? Your father's?"

"My grandfather's."

When the meat was done cooking, the boys went back inside. They walked into the kitchen and Trevor hugged his fiance. Carlos put the plate of meat on the countertop. The next couple hours were full of the four college students talking to Mrs. Allen, laughing over stories of Olivia's childhood.

Eventually, Mr. Allen came home. He gave his daughter a big hug and whispered something in her ear which made her laugh. Then he reached over to shake Carlos and Trevor's hands. Olivia and Abby went to the back of the house to their room, in an attempt to find something for each of them to wear.

Around that time, Mrs. Allen's aunt came through the door. She was tall and beautiful and had a strong personality. She had short grey hair and glasses.

"Hi, Aunt Gail!" Mrs. Allen said as she moved to greet her.

"Hey, Gail," Mr. Allen said with a slight wave.

"Hidy, Deborah! Hi, Robert!" she said as she hugged her niece, Mrs. Allen. "Where's Olivia?"

"She and her friend are getting ready. In the meantime, I'd like you to meet Carlos."

"Hidy, Carlos!" he waved back.

"And Olivia's fiance, Trevor."

"Hello, Mrs. Gail."

She looked him over for a moment as she slowly shook his hand. Finally, she asked, "What's your last name son?"

"It's Foster."

Gail smiled. Trevor thought she was probably imagining Olivia as a Foster. That's when Olivia ran out of her room in a purple sundress that came to the floor.

"Hi aunt Gail!" she said.

"How you doin' O?" she asked as she hugged Olivia.

"I'm fine. How's Uncle?"

"He's fine. Off on business again. You wouldn't think anyone else in the world was a youth pastor/missionary by the way they work him."

Trevor looked at Carlos who seemed to be thinking about something. He shook his head slightly as if to say 'That's ridiculous'.

"Have you met Trevor yet?" Olivia asked as she grabbed his arm and he waved.

"Yep, we were just introduced."

"Good! Well, this is my friend Abby."

"Hello, Mrs. Gail."

"It's very nice to meet you." She looked at Abby's bright blue eyes for a second, "I hope you don't mind my asking, but is your full name, Abigail?"

"Yes ma'am. Abigail Davidson."

Gail smiled, the same one she'd done towards Trevor. "Mhmm. Very nice, dear."

Trevor thought something was up with that woman, he just didn't know what.

Not long after, they began the festivities. Mrs. Allen brought all the food into their living room and set it on the coffee table. They had music playing through a little radio that sat on the mantle. After an hour or so, Trevor sat on the grey sectional couch and watched it all. Abby sat next to him.

"You ok?"

Trevor sighed. "Yeah. It would've been nice if he had come, you know?"

Abby leaned back on her chair, insinuating that she wasn't moving any time soon. They watched everyone eating, talking, and having fun.

"Olivia seems happy, doesn't she?"

"Yeah," Trevor answered, smiling. "Wait, is that Carlos' third hamburger?"

Carlos looked over at him with a mouthful, "No…" he said wide-eyed, mouth filled.

Abby laughed, "Your best friend is hilarious, Trev."

"When are you going to get together with ol' hamburger addict over there?"

Trevor thought Abby's cheeks turned a little pink. "Oh, I-"

"Listen up everybody," Mrs. Allen said as she tapped her water glass with a spoon, "Olivia told me that Trevor already proposed to her, but she said she would have to wait for her father's permission. Well, her father gave permission. As far as I know, Olivia hasn't said yes yet. Trevor, I think you need to re-propose now that there's a larger chance of getting a positive answer out of her."

Trevor smiled as he put his head in his hands. Everyone started saying different things and clapping in an attempt to get him to come to the front of the room. Abby patted him on the back. Trevor looked up and walked forward. He grabbed both of Olivia's hands.

"Olivia."

"Yes?"

"Wait!" Gail said. She took a ring from her pointer finger. "You might have a better chance of a yes if it comes with a rock," she winked. "It was my mother's."

She dropped a beautiful diamond ring with a golden band into Trevor's palm. He mouthed the words "thank you" to Gail and she winked. Trevor's gaze went back to Olivia.

"Olivia, I-"

Over his girlfriend's shoulder, he saw the door open. He moved his head to the right a bit to see who it was. He felt a smile come across his face.

"Dad."

Eighteen

The Travel Book

6/30/1980

Dear Katherine,

I'm packing up my clothes right now! I can't wait to see you! It feels like it's been forever since I saw you last. I can't wait to be home. I've been missing you a lot. I've barely slept the past few nights because I was so excited to see you. Believe me, it's true. I'm not just saying that to make you feel like I'm sweet or something. I mean, we all know that I AM sweet, but I wasn't making that particular section up to intensify my sweetness. What? You weren't thinking that? Wow, Kat, we really need to work on your complimenting skills.

So, Colonel Moore came to the barracks to say goodbye to me earlier. I was pulling my suitcase out of my locker. He was standing a couple of yards behind me. I turned around and immediately dropped my bag and stood in attention.

"Don't worry about it, Sanders. Pick up your bag."

"Yes sir," I said as I bent down to get my bag. "Is it ok if I do a little bit of packing while you're in here?"

"Oh yeah, go ahead."

"Thanks."

I began grabbing some of my clothes and tossing them in my bag. He started rubbing the back of his neck and taking little, nervous steps forward.

"Are you ok, Colonel?"

"Yeah. I just wanted to apologize again for how I treated you when you first got here."

"Oh, you don't have-"

"Sanders, please. You didn't deserve my disrespect. I was a jerk. And you were in a new place. I shouldn't have treated you that way."

"Sir, really-"

"Truth is, I was feeling bad about myself. I missed the birth of my kids, both of them, because of my job. My wife said she didn't mind. She said she honestly didn't want me to see her yelling and being in pain the way she was. I've only seen my youngest child once."

"I'm sorry. At least she knows how much you regret it."

"When I saw you come in, a newlywed, excited about your job, I guess I was just jealous. I wasn't having the best time in MY job and I guess, in my head, I thought everyone else deserved to hate their job in the Army too."

"Colonel Moore, it's ok. You apologized already. You actually gave me a chance to rethink how I handled certain situations. Your apology to me told me that I was doing something right."

"That's great and all, bu-"

"Uh, excuse me for interrupting, Colonel, but I really need to say this. Sometimes, when people do things they are not proud of, the only person that doesn't forgive them is themselves. You asked for my forgiveness and I gave it to you. You no longer have to feel guilty on my behalf. The only thing it's doing is hurting yourself. I've forgiven you, God's forgiven you-"

"God? You're a Christian Sanders?"

I was taken aback. "Yes sir. I thought you were from that apology you gave me. Are you not?"

"No. I don't even believe in God."

"Well, I hate to break it to you Colonel, but I think He's already with you," I said, smiling as I turned back to my locker.

"You think He's with me?" he asked, taking a couple of steps forward.

"I do, and if you ask, I'm positive He'll stay."

"How do you know? How do you know He's really with me?"

"Because you apologized to me for something you were embarrassed about. Apologies are one of the hardest things in the world to give. It takes in-human strength to apologize for something the way you did. God wouldn't let you try to do it alone." I then turned to my locker. I pulled out my Bible and turned back around and started to give it to Colonel Moore.

"Oh, I couldn't take your book."

"It's ok, Colonel. This is just my travel one. I have more at my dad's house. Take it. If I were you, I'd start with Matthew. If you read that, you won't have a doubt about God being with you."

He reached his hands out slowly and grabbed it. He flipped through the pages and looked it over.

"I hope it's ok that I've highlighted some of the verses in there," I said.

"Oh no, it's fine. It'll help me find some good ones to read." He took his gaze from the book to me. "Thank you, soldier. You are much appreciated."

"I should be thanking you! I could not have gotten that job back home if it weren't for you. I appreciate you, Colonel Moore."

"Say hello to your wife and baby for me."

"I'll do that," I said. We smiled at each other and then Colonel Moore left.

I never would've dreamed that I would come to like Colonel Moore as much as I do. I mean, my worst enemy from the first bit I was here in Turkey, has now become the memory of my work here that I'm the fondest of. Besides Anderson of course. Speaking of Anderson, I haven't seen him in a while. I wanted to say goodbye to him, but when I went to find him, the other chefs said he had taken a vacation. I was kind of disappointed, but I hope he's having fun.

Anyway, I should probably get back to packing. I am so very very excited to see you, Katherine! It won't be long!

Love,

Ronnie

Nineteen

To Trevor and Olivia!

"*A*m I too late? If there's still cake left I'm not terribly late," Mr. Foster said, smiling. Trevor forgot how much he missed that smile until he saw it again.

"We haven't even cut the cake yet, sir! You must be Mr. Foster," Olivia's father said, laughing as he walked towards him, "I'm Robert Allen."

"Nice to meet you, Mr. Allen."

"Would you like some punch?" Mrs. Allen asked. "Trevor was just getting ready to re-propose to Olivia."

"Oh, he was? Well, don't let me hold you up!" Mr. Foster said as he plopped into the chair next to the door.

"Thanks, dad." Trevor just couldn't seem to get the smile off of his face. He turned back around and grabbed his girlfriend's hands again. "Olivia, I love you with everything in me. I love you more than I thought I could love anybody and it is an amazing feeling. I never want to imagine a life without you. You inspire me every day to be somebody extraordinary just like you. So," he knelt and held up the ring, "do you wanna get married?"

"Yes, Trevor Foster, I believe I do."

Trevor smiled at her ever-present country accent. He stood up and slid the ring on Olivia's finger. They spent the next few seconds awkwardly looking at each other. Trevor wasn't sure if he was allowed to kiss her in front of her family.

"Oh, give her a smooch, boy!" Gail hollered from the back of the room.

The room filled with laughter as the two sealed their deal. Mr. Foster seemed to be the happiest of anybody. When Mrs. Allen went to the front of the room to ask if anybody wanted to make a toast, his hand shot up. As Mr. Foster walked to the front of the room, Trevor started to get a little nervous.

"Hi everybody. I'm Trevor's father, Eric. I-uh-well, I don't usually do this sort of thing, but this is good practice for the wedding I guess. Um, well, I guess I'll start with a little story. When Trevor was a baby, his mother, Melony, and I had a fight. A big one. We got divorced pretty early on in our marriage. Luckily, Trevor still had a healthy relationship with his mom.

We both still love her, she's an incredible person, it just didn't work out the way we had planned. He grew up mostly with me.

"Well, anyways, his mom was always the one with more money. When she left, I didn't have much, so we had to move to a more rundown part of the city. I told Trevor that there weren't many good people there and, believe me, there weren't. The only way to keep him safe was to tell him not to talk to anybody. To keep his head down and trust no-one. I taught him about the realities of the world. About murders and abuse and other things. I taught him how to fight, to defend himself.

"I had to work a lot when we lived there, to keep the lights on. I was so overwhelmed by my work that I didn't realize how distant he was becoming. How much the realities that I had warned him about, maybe a little too often, were consuming him. Destroying him. He had no friends and trusted absolutely nobody and it was my fault. I won't blame anybody or anything else for that, it was me and for that, I am so sorry. He was so defensive all the time. It took him years to open himself up again, and it wasn't to me. It was to Melony's parents, Katherine and Ron.

"They taught him how to love and how to make friends again. How to trust and not conspire. He started going to their house more and more. Eventually, Trevor got old enough for high school, and that's where he met Carlos. They were best friends from the beginning. Slowly, he started to become a person again. I was so glad he was opening up, even if I wasn't there long enough for him to confide in me.

"Despite my many mistakes in parenting, Trevor turned out to be an incredible young man. He is so mature and strong and loves so many. I am very proud of you, son.

"He taught me something though, and maybe you can use

this in your life. Children, well, people in general, will have enough earth-shattering experiences in their lives. They will be betrayed, and heartbroken, and scared, just like we all have. There are too many horrific experiences in a person's life for fear to be the topic of conversation at the dinner table. Let your conversations follow love, peace, joy, and all the other wonderful gifts that have been given to us.

"Remind yourselves of all the fantastic experiences that can happen in the world. The wonderful things that have happened in the world. In Trevor's small circle of friends, I can tell that they do this together. One of the most important things in the world is to have people beside you, reminding you of the realities that are more real and more bright than any scary experiences that all of us have had.

"Now, Olivia, I don't know you very well, but if my son likes you, then, well, I guess I like you too. Just don't make the mistake I did. Be there for him. Love on him. Remind him of the reality of love that the world neglects to remember. The reality my son and I forgot.

"There is absolutely no better gift, and I mean no better gift than the gift of time. The two of you are young and getting married. Just don't forget about that simple little gift, no matter how busy life may get. It costs less than nothing and means more than anything. Good luck with your marriage you two. I know you'll do fine. To Trevor and Olivia!" he said as he raised his glass.

"To Trevor and Olivia!" the crowd echoed.

Everyone clapped as Trevor walked to the front of the room. He wrapped his arms around his father for the first time since…

well, he didn't remember. Mr. Foster hugged him back.

"I love you, kid. I'm sorry I never told you."

"I love you too, dad."

Trevor could've stayed in that house, in that room, in that happiness forever. He never wanted to leave. The two men walked back and sat on the couch. Mrs. Allen stood up and gave her speech to the bride. Gail came and sat next to Mr. Foster. Trevor was dying to know what the two of them were over there whispering about. He'd probably never find out. He shrugged it off and kept listening to Mrs. Allen's speech.

At the end of the night, Gail left, and eventually, Mr. Foster followed. Trevor walked him out.

"I want to apologize to you for all those times I yelled at you," Mr. Foster said. "All those times I showed up and acted disappointed in you. All those times I just…acted like an idiot. Trevor, I was never mad at you. I've always loved you. In all honesty, I was mad at myself. I was never there for you when you needed me. I wanted to be with you, but somehow, every time I saw you it reminded me of all those parenting mistakes I'd made. It was never you, kid. I was never disappointed in you. I've always been very proud of you. I just wasn't good at showing it."

"Dad, it's ok. I forgive you. You tried your best with me. I've never thought otherwise. All of us could be better at everything we do. That toast in there proved that you are becoming a better father."

Mr. Foster smiled and looked in the window at Trevor's friends, laughing as they helped Mrs. Allen clean up. "You've got some good people in there, Trev."

"They are. They really are."

They waited in the warm silence for a moment. Trevor looked towards his father.

"What are you thinking about?" he asked.

"I just can't believe my little boy is going to tie the knot!" Mr. Foster answered as he playfully smacked him in the arm.

"It is weird isn't it?"

"Yeah, but a good weird."

"The best," Trevor answered.

"I love you kid; you know that?"

"I do now," Trevor replied, grinning from ear to ear.

They hugged again and Mr. Foster went home. The next day, Trevor, Olivia, Carlos, and Abby went back to the campus, all of them just a little bit closer than they were when they left. Olivia and Trevor were married in a matter of months. It was quaint. just close family, but they couldn't have asked for anything better. They were ready for new adventures and they'd experience them together.

Trevor had a very successful year as a junior in college. During the summer, he began his job as a mechanic and was extremely good at it. He was able to provide for and bless his family more than he would have dreamed. He was there for them when they needed him, just as they had always been there for him. Nothing made him happier.

Twenty

A Proud Daddy's Letter

5/4/1980

Dear Mary,

I can't believe I'm a father. I can't believe I've been a father for all of thirty minutes! I can't believe you're my daughter. There's a whole lot of things I'm having a hard time believing.

Your mother is exhausted and asleep on her hospital bed. She's so brave, Mary. She's going to be a great mom.

Anyway, I thought this could be a chance for the two of us to get to know one another. I'm holding you with my left hand and writing this letter with my right. You're so tiny. I've never seen a baby this tiny before. And beautiful too. You've changed my life forever and you don't even know it yet.

I can't believe I was nervous about this. At this particular moment, I can't remember why. All I can think about is how excited I am for you to grow up with me. I've still got a long way to go. Maybe not as long as you have, but I am, definitely, still growing up.

I just want you to know that today, right now, you have done nothing too special. You've cried a little and slept a lot. You lie here, occasionally sticking your tongue out. So, little Mary, before you succeed and before you fail, I love you very very much. You've done nothing to deserve it, nothing to earn it, and yet, somehow, I love you more than I've ever loved any kid out there.

And before you do something that will make me mad, and before you do something extraordinary, I want you to know that I'm proud of you. I could have never asked for anybody better, and I've only known you for thirty minutes!

Now I want you to know that we're both going to make mistakes. You AND me. But we have to remember how much we love each other and how hard we're BOTH trying. I will probably let you down, I'll probably yell at you for something you didn't do, but I want you to know how much I don't want to. Mary, I'm afraid it's unavoidable.

But, on the days when sin seems a little farther from our house, in the moments when it seems that nothing could be better, I'll teach you about what is even more real than anger and sin and hurt. I'll remind you of things that mistakes can't take away.

I'll remind you of love. Nothing either of us could do would make me love you any less than I do right this second. Nothing anybody could do would make me want to forget this moment: holding you in this extremely uncomfortable little hospital chair. Love is more real than anything you will ever face, Mary. It requires closeness and hope. Paul, from the Bible, says that the greatest thing of all is love. You can't get much more bluntly wise than that.

While you lie here, sleeping on my arm, I'm imagining all of the fun we're about to have. All the times you're not going to laugh at my terrible jokes. All the times you're going to say my name when you need help. All the times I'm going to play with you.

When you get a little older, you can play with my good friend Anderson too. He used some of his vacation days to come to Virginia and see you be born. He is a really good friend. One day, you'll make a friend as incredibly amazing as him. I can't wait.

You're a pretty important little girl, and you're only half an hour old!

Life's an opportunity, Mary. Whatever you decide to do, I will be right behind you, remembering the day you came into the world, looking like a mix between a tiny human and a pink raisin. I'm kidding! I'm kidding! Sort of. Ha ha.....ha?

Well, I guess I already made my first lame joke. And you were asleep! You missed it! Rats! Well, there will be plenty more where that came from. And I'll be right here to tell you them all.

I love you Mary Linn Sanders and I always will.

Your proud daddy,

Ron

Twenty-One

Fast Forward

*T*wo years later.

Trevor went through the automatic doors, pushing his shopping cart full of the bags of ice he had purchased. He looked to make sure no cars were coming before he went back to his small, silver vehicle. That's when a dark grey SUV drove in front of him and stopped. The window slowly rolled down.

"Hi, Grandma and Grandpa!" Trevor exclaimed.

"Hi, Trevor!" Grandma said, just as excited, "Abby told us you were at the store. We thought we'd drive by and see if we could catch you."

"Holy cow Trevor, what do you need all that ice for?" Grandpa asked.

"It's for the party after Abby's graduation. Are you guys coming?"

"We wouldn't miss it! Do you want to ride with us to the college?"

"Um, sure. I'll drive back up here with Carlos and get my car. Can I put the ice in your trunk?"

"Sure!"

Trevor placed the bags into the trunk and jumped in the car.

"I can't believe Abigail is graduating!" Grandma said.

"I know," Trevor answered, "it's insane."

"And you and Olivia are about to have an anniversary aren't you?"

"Yeah. Three years ago next month, I asked her on our first date."

"Wait, I thought you'd been married three years?" Grandpa asked.

"Nope, just been together. We've been married for two years."

"Ah, ok."

"How's the baby?" Grandma asked. She was, of course, referring to Trevor junior. The spitting image of his father. About a year and a half into their marriage, Olivia gave birth to the most incredible baby boy. Of course, her opinion may be a little biased.

"He's fine. Getting into trouble as always."

"Oh those kids," Grandpa said as he turned the steering wheel to the left.

"And your father?"

Trevor smiled, "He's good. We went fishing the day before yesterday. He caught more than me."

A couple of years ago, a question like that would have caused his palms to start sweating. He would've wanted to change the subject. He would not have known how his father was. He was so happy that they were close. He had always wanted the father he now had.

"Are you still working at the mechanic's shop?" Grandpa asked.

"Yes, sir. Carlos is letting me handle the English speakers more than the Spanish speakers. I'm still studying Spanish. I need some serious help. One guy came in and he didn't know how to speak English. I tried to tell him that he needed new tires, but I accidentally told him to go bathe his pig." Trevor got some laughs out of that one.

The three drove in silence for a moment before Grandma told her husband,

"You know, you always do that."

"Do what?" Grandpa asked.

"When we're driving straight forward for a long time, you put your left wrist on the steering wheel and rub your mustache with your right hand."

"No, I don't!" he quipped, pulling his right hand off of his mustache.

"Yes you do, Grandpa," Trevor said through a chuckle.

"I don't know what you guys are talking about."

"It's cute!" Grandma said, laughing.

"Oh, everybody's a comedian!" Grandpa said.

The drive didn't last much longer. Trevor enjoyed every moment of it. Being with his grandparents made him feel like a kid no matter how old he was. He looked around inside the car. He found the regular stuff. A road map from ten years ago or more, a sudoku puzzle book, a nail file, an umbrella with a wooden duck head on the handle.

Finally, he came across a little piece of paper. It looked like it had been cut out of a magazine. Trevor had always remembered it being on the fridge when he was a kid. It was purple with white words on it. 'Yesterday is history; Tomorrow, a mystery; But today is a gift. That's why it's called the present.'

"This was on the floor back here, Grandma," Trevor said, reaching it over her shoulder.

"Oh thank you. I've been looking for this. I meant to put it back on the fridge."

All of a sudden, as if he'd been struck by lightning and was abruptly being transported to a different time, Trevor had a flashback to his childhood. It was as if he was Scrooge from that book *A Christmas Carol*. The memory was so vivid. It was dinner time. He was seven years old. Grandpa was asleep in his recliner in the living room. Trevor tiptoed into the kitchen, careful not to wake him. His grandmother was there, stirring something in a bowl. He didn't know what.

"Hi, buddy. Is Grandpa asleep?"

"Yeah."

"Don't you mean yes ma'am, Trevor?" she said, sweetly stern.

"Yes ma'am."

He climbed into the little barstool in the kitchen. Of course, at the time, it seemed like the tallest chair known to man and he was proud when he made it up. He looked at all the pictures and magnets on the fridge next to him. He could tell Grandma was smiling behind him as he looked up and down the refrigerator.

He saw a little purple piece of paper with his grandmother's favorite quote on it.

"Grandma? Why do you have that piece of paper?"

"Well, it reminds me of something very important. Every section of it. 'Yesterday is history' reminds me of the fact that yesterday is gone. All those times I messed up, all those times I'm not proud of are not here anymore. You know your history class?"

"Yes ma'am."

"Well, that part about history reminds me that I can learn from my mistakes and my victories, just like you learn about all those people in your history book. 'Tomorrow a mystery' reminds me of all the spectacular possibilities that are coming for me. It reminds me of all the amazing things I'm going to do in my life. 'But today is a gift' reminds me to love today. Today is the day the Lord has made. There's a reason today came and I was here. I mean, gifts are good things meant for our delight. God gave me today for no reason at all, except for the fact that He loves me. Isn't that amazing, Trevor?"

'Tomorrow a mystery,' Trevor murmured, still slightly caught in the memory. 'Spectacular possibilities are coming for me. Isn't that amazing?'

Acknowledgments

Oh wow. There are so many people that I would love to "acknowledge" on this small page. So many mentors, inspirations, piers, and leaders I'd love to mention. Of course, I want to thank my grandparents once again for their time, patience, and stories. They are the inspiration for Katherine and Ron Sanders. I'd also like to thank my very amazing friend and former youth pastor Sarah, who continues to point out God's simple beauty in every corner of my life. And then there are all the wonderfully sweet people at my church who supported me both financially and verbally. Your encouragement was what pushed me to write another story. Most importantly, I would like to thank my incredible family. My mom helps me with the editing/grammar-correcting portion of the book. Trust me, these things would be a train wreck without her hard work. My dad helps me with the publishing portion of the work. Without his help, you would not be holding this book in your hand. And then there's my brother who is always so engaged in my wacky ideas. I couldn't have done it without you guys! God's love has taken over our lives; His faithful ways are eternal!-Psalm 117:2
:)

Also by Graci Lowe

Graci Lowe's books are always centered around faith, love, and relationships. They were written for kids anywhere from eight to one hundred and eight years old. She hopes to share the knowledge that the Lord Jesus Christ is in our schools, our jobs, our towns, and our friendships. Enjoy, book fans!

Yesterday is History

Abigail Davidson begins college with a whole lot of doubts. With the help of her grandmother's journal from her army days, she is able to find hope, guidance, and some of the answers she's been looking for. Of course, she does make some friends along the way.

www.ingramcontent.com/pod-product-compliance
Lightning Source LLC
Chambersburg PA
CBHW052017150726
47999CB00004B/1695